MW00959572

COWARDLY
as a
LION

KENDRA MORENO

Copyright © 2021 by Kendra Moreno

All rights reserved.

No part of this book may be reproduced in any form or by any electronic or mechanical means, including information storage and retrieval systems, without written permission from the author, except for the use of brief quotations in a book review.

PLEASE DO NOT PIRATE, PIRATES SUCK.

Cover artwork by: Ashley Walters
Cover Typography by: Methyss Art
Formatting by: The Nutty Formatter

*This book is for everyone who has ever looked into the darkness and
violently came back into the light.
Healing is fucking messy, and look at you,
a Goddess rising.*

We are all wolves, and we will howl together.

PROLOGUE

There's nothing I can do about what had been done except to do my part as an Heir and retreat to my domain. The lobo has been locked up in Emerald City for the foreseeable future, imprisoned by the three of us in the hopes that one day, we can address the problem. It's humbling to realize that the Tin man, the Scarecrow, and I aren't powerful enough to defeat Toto, only lock him away. Even locking him away had taken something from us, and we couldn't have done it alone. No, we had to have the help of the witch currently near death in my arms.

Azalea had used nearly all of her power to cast the spell. She'd paid a heavier price than us, and for that, we owe her far more than we could give. Though I had given up something important, I can still recognize precisely what she'd done for Oz. We had to give up a piece to save our world; Azalea had to give up everything.

My leg is injured to the point of agony. Before we'd figured out we couldn't win, we had tried to fight Toto. It should have been easy enough to kill the werewolf, however, Toto is not just that at all. He's a lobo, a werewolf capable of wielding magic. A threat so large shouldn't be allowed to exist, let alone left to destroy as much as he had. It was all because Dorothy had found the beast and walked him right inside our doors. None of us even know where the monster came from. I only hope there aren't more to follow.

The shreds in my leg will serve as a reminder. I'm difficult to kill —we all are—but I will bear the scars on my skin where the meat hangs loose from bone. By all intents and purposes, I shouldn't be able to walk, but I'm no weakling. I'm an Heir, the Lion, and King of Winkie Country. The least I can do is show it.

Azalea stirs in my arms as I travel through the outskirts of Emerald City until I reach Quadling County. This quarters of Oz belongs to no one, a neutral space left to its own devices. The Wicked Witch had chosen it has her home once her troublesome sister caused a stir and disappeared. The Good Witch had been the complete opposite of Azalea. Where Azalea is less evil than her name implies, her sister had been not an ounce of good. I never understood how their roles were reversed in the world, but I thought it only good propaganda on the Good Witch's part. Azalea may be the Wicked Witch of Oz, but she had done more for Oz than the fucking Good Witch had ever done. When her sister disappeared, it had been a relief. I don't even care if she'd died somewhere in a hole. The woman was a terror.

Azalea's home appears out of the trees as I stumble through the brush and decaying trees. As we walk through, the trees seem to come back to life, as if just having Azalea back in the forest is all the heart it needs. Too bad the Tin Man can't do the same after all this.

"What. . ."

Looking down at the witch in my arms, I grunt when she tried to speak.

"You should save your strength." My own voice comes out just as strained, the pain of my leg seeping into my speech. Once I get Azalea settled, I'll need to retreat to my domain to lick my wounds. Healing is going to be a painful process.

Her eyes roll up, too much white in her gaze, until they land on her cottage rising up out of the trees like a phantom. Realization hits her. Had she expected us to leave her where she lay? I like to think the three of us Heirs have more honor than that, however, I'm not sure we do. I'm taking Azalea to her home out of respect for what she'd done.

We may be villains. We may be evil. But not a single one of us are completely heartless.

Well. . .I suppose now the Tin Man is. . .

"You brought me back," she rasps, her head so heavy, she can barely lift it enough to look at me.

I look like a nightmare. I know I'm completely covered in blood and gore, not to mention I'm literally walking with meat hanging from my thigh. My hair alternates between blood-soaked and ratted. There's blood dried around my mouth from where I'd bitten Toto in the shoulder. I'm not pleasant to look at right now, yet Azalea doesn't flinch away.

She lacks the physical harm that the Heirs all suffered, except for exhaustion from running. Azalea wasn't bitten or clawed by Toto. Instead, her weakness comes from within. Locking Toto away had taken something from her core, but she won't tell us what. Maybe not even she knows.

"You thought we'd just let you die after everything?" I grunt. My leg is starting to drag, my strength to move it running out. Soon, I won't have a choice but to collapse where I stand.

"Yes," she says, her tone so matter of fact, I realize she believed that completely. My only answer is a grunt of displeasure, but I don't argue. I'm not a good person, though I do my best to take care of my people. Tin and Crow are the same. We're not meant for niceties. We're simply meant to rule and keep Oz from descending into chaos.

Her sunset eyes brighten the closer I limp to her home, as if the source of her power is inside. Perhaps, it is. I can't say I know much about the Wicked Witch other than her ability to cast spells and cause mischief if she needs to.

"Why?" she asks.

I scoff. "Why what?"

I have enough strength to look down in her eyes, but whatever I see there unnerves me. She sees too much, understands things at a whole differently level.

"Your empathy. . ."

"Is an unnecessary emotion." I grit my teeth against a sharp bite of pain that nearly has my knee collapsing. Only pure willpower keeps it from failing completely. "If I'm to keep Toto locked away, then I don't need empathy. That'll only serve as a threat to his prison."

"We all need empathy to live."

"I'm alive right now," I growl back, ever the asshole. I can't say I've ever gotten along much with the Wicked Witch but having her question my reasoning only pisses me off more. "Clearly, I didn't need it."

She doesn't speak again until I'm kicking in the tiny door to her cottage, and only then, it's mostly a sound of displeasure as the hinges groan at my entrance. I'm hardly gentle enough to be considered nice, but she doesn't complain when I drop her on the tiny couch pressed against the wall. Dust wafts into the air around her, as if she doesn't ever clean the damned house, but I'm not her maid. If she wants a dirty house, that's her problem.

"Good luck," I grunt, and turn to leave, determined to make it as close to possible to Winkie Country before I collapse. If I can at least make it inside my domain, I'll be safe from anyone who may touch me. My own people won't dare.

"King," Azalea calls, making me freeze just as I stoop to go back out the door. The wooden panel hangs at an odd angle now because of my aggression but I don't feel any regret for that. I can't. Not anymore.

"Yes?"

"Just because you're living doesn't mean you're alive," she whispers. My shoulders tense, but she doesn't add anymore wisdom to that. Instead, she gestures to a large bottle on the counter beside the door. "Take that with you. Put it on your wound for the next three days."

I don't question it. I may not be able to empathize with the witch, but I've long since learned to take her advice. I gently take the bottle in my hand, and then, because I feel the need to leave payment, I reach into the coin purse at my hip and draw a large green emerald, a piece of the castle at the center of Oz, and drop it on the table. Her eyes widen, but I don't wait for her response. It means nothing now. Once, it would have been worth everything.

I limp out of the door, close it behind me despite the damaged hinges, and push myself forward on a leg mostly stripped of muscle until I literally can't go anymore. I collapse right inside the border of Winkie Country, just at the edge of safety.

It takes me three days to move again. . .

CHAPTER ONE

FERAL

The trees fly passed me, great massive carnivorous things that won't hesitate to eat me should I pause for longer than two seconds. I'm sporting a large nick out of my right flank where a large fly trap plant decided to taste me. I'd ripped it to shreds for the slight, leaving behind a nice pile of leaves and greenery. I never knew plants could scream, but they do in this world, whatever world this is that I've found myself in.

The path of the prey I hunt suddenly swerves to the left, an attempt to lose me off course, but the creature is foolish. No matter its direction, I can smell its scent from a mile away. Of course, it's a new trick I've learned. Before, I couldn't hunt something by smell alone. Before, I couldn't pick up a drop of blood from the other side of a territory. Before. . .

Who was I before? Sometimes, I forget that I wasn't always this great hulking beast of a creature. Sometimes, I forget that I had a life that was once more than hunting and running. Now, it's all I know. I don't know how long it's been since I last walked on my own two legs. I don't know how long it's been since Perry—

I shut down the thought hard, shoving it back into my memory until the wolf takes over and reminds me that I'm hunting prey. I need to eat, this body requiring far more sustenance than I'm used to. The prey is smarter in this world, but it doesn't stop me from catching meals. I just have to be fast enough to catch them. This one at least smells warm-blooded. The one creature I hunted before this was made of glass, safe from me as dinner. I couldn't have bitten the cat if I wanted to. It was far smarter than other prey and I suspected I didn't catch it as much as it caught me. Still, we'd both walked around each other hesitantly and went our separate ways. I haven't seen the glass cat again.

The creature running from me smells like the piss stink of fear and the ripest strawberries. I don't know what it is, but when I catch sight of it through the trees, it's made up of rectangles and squares. Its sides are flat rather than curved like a proper animal. All sides of it are flat-sided and planed, perfectly at ninety-degree angles. It gives it a strange appearance as it runs, as if it's not physically meant to. Still, the thing is fast.

A savage snarl peels my lips back as I chase it, gaining on the creature desperately trying to get away. It screeches at me when it turns to see how close I am and realizes I'm closing in. My stomach gives an excited gurgle for the meal I'm about to eat.

"Leave woozy alone!" the creature screams, making me stumble for a split second. I hadn't expected the creature to be sentient, but my hunger outweighs my humanity. I need to feed or else I'm going to die. Unfortunately for the creature, it's been unlucky enough to cross my path.

"Food," I growl, lengthening my strides at the prospect of a satisfying meal. My voice doesn't even sound like me anymore. It's all beast.

"Woozy not food!" The thing tries to push itself faster, but I can see it struggling to maintain the speed. It's exhausted, the square legs not meant to run for such an extended period of time. "Not food! Not food! Woozy good!"

The words penetrate my mind, but I've pushed so much out for so long, it's not hard to shove it deep. I can't afford to feel empathy for a creature I have to eat. I can't afford to starve. I still have business to tend to.

What was the business? Why can't I remember my name? My name is. . .

"Not food!" the thing screeches as I barrel through the trees and outstretch my claws, inches away from its hindquarters. "Please! Not food!"

My claws rip into the hard planes of the creature's hips and the scream of pure panic it lets out threatens to shatter my ear drums as I take it to the ground. It struggles in my hold, keening high and low as its square face peers into mine. My lips peel back over my teeth, baring them for the creature as I drag it to me. It fights helplessly against my powerful hold, struggling, crying. Is it crying?

"Please don't eat woozy! Woozy not food!"

Regret hits me but I'm more beast than human, and with a savage growl, I clamp my jaws around its throat, cutting off air supply. I feel the soft tissue crunch, and the creature struggles for a few seconds more, its words cutting off in a bloody gurgle. It falls limp against me, too intelligent eyes rolling back in its head. I have the sudden realization I've killed something that wasn't as much a creature as I thought, that it might have been more human than I am, but I'm hungry, and hunger makes all creatures equal.

Still, as I tear into the somehow soft flesh of the creature, true regret fills me. Once upon a time, I was a moral person. I didn't harm those who didn't harm me. If I hunted, I did so out of necessity and never filled a creature with such fear, it begged me to let it live. This isn't me. This isn't who I am.

Unfortunately, I can barely remember who I once was so long ago.

Yellow blood smears across my face as I tear into the soft innards of the creature, as I eat as much as possible before the plant life decides to move in to scavenge what I can't finish. Sometimes, it doesn't wait for me to finish. Sometimes, it tries to fight. I prefer to avoid confrontation with things that can't truly be harmed in a way that will satisfy me. After all, what's the point?

With my belly full and my heart heavy, I back away from the creature growing cold on the ground. I'm panting, not because of the run, but because of the sadness that threatens to overtake me. I don't want to be like this. I don't want to feel such pain, but I'm just a beast now. What had I even looked like before the change?

The color red flashes across my vision, but I don't know what it means, what it pertains to. Why is red an important color?

A scent of something wafts passed my nose, something that passed through this path recently. It's large, a predator, masculine. What is it?

My whole-body tenses at the perceived threat with the scent, as if something has encroached on my territory. But none of this is mine. None of this world is mine. I shouldn't be territorial, but something about the scent makes me want to find it. The hackles on the back of my neck rise.

I'm feral as I turn in the direction of the smell. I'm always feral. I don't know what my name was before I'd claimed Feral as a name. It dances on the edge of my mind, but my beast chases it away in favor of the scent.

Find it, she purrs. *Find him.*

And because I'm little more than instinct and savagery, I listen.

With a great howl, I begin to run after the scent trail, hunting, hunting. . .

I know nothing else. . .

CHAPTER TWO

KING

Winkie Country makes up the east quarter of Oz. It's been my domain for as long as I can remember. Other worlds know of a moment they become their role, but in Oz, we came into existence and know nothing before it. I don't remember a time where I wasn't an Heir. I don't remember ever being younger than I am now. Perhaps, we're not born, but created.

Where the other realms are all made up differently, Winkie Country has its own atmosphere and characteristics. Tin's realm is all cybernetics and city. Crow's is empty save for the howling souls of the dead. Quadling County is mostly quiet, though it's louder nowadays with the worlds merging. Azalea has spoken of some of the new things she'd witnessed in her realm along with her new sidekick. She'd described the castle that our newest threat had woken from, and I'm glad it didn't encroach into Winkie Country. I would have preferred it not find its way into Oz at all.

My realm is far more poisonous than the others. The plant life here is hungry and angry, and the inhabitants make up diverse types of creatures. Most of them can kill a human easily, simply my spitting at them. Some of them are so dangerous, they choose to live in the darkest parts of the forest where no one ever sees them. Those are the only ones I enforce my position over because if they roam, they can cause just as much destruction as a lobo, and they wouldn't even mean to.

Not that I care anymore what they do.

Since Toto was locked away, I've cared less and less. I no longer enforce most rules. Instead, I take a hands-off approach and only step in if necessary. I don't care anymore, but I'm aware enough to know logical solutions to problems. Sometimes, I have to step in to keep the balance, not because I care people will die, but because it's my job.

Where Tin's world is all electronics and neon, my world is the complete opposite. Winkie Country is like stepping back into time where knights rode into battle against dragons, or so I've been told. The Flamingo, when he came to Oz so long ago, told me of such stories. Though he's back in Oz with the other new creatures here staying in Tin's territory, I haven't had time to ask him for more stories. Oz was once his home, but the entire time the Flamingo was here, he was fighting to get back to the woman he spoke of as often as he breathed.

At the time, I'd wondered what it would be like to love something so much.

Now, I can barely understand the concept.

With two locks of Toto's prison released because of the emotion, I can't say I'm eager to find out, even if there's talks of some sort of prophesy. No one speaks my destiny. No one decides my fate for me. There's no way my empathy can be returned to me without my choice in the matter, and so Toto will be locked away. We only have to worry about the threat of the other World Breakers and the menace that is Rumpelstiltskin. Perhaps, we'll stand a chance against them when they decide to show their faces again. But Toto was hard enough to lock away the first time. Though we're stronger now and have more people, I can't say I have full faith in our ability to overcome a lobo teaming up with a World Breaker.

Though Emerald City glitters menacingly in the distance, the color shining more than it had been before, it's not the only castle in Oz. My own home is a smaller stone castle, a beautiful construct that I choose to reside in. I *am* a King, after all. Not just an Heir.

"We'll face Toto again."

I ignore the voice because it's the way I operate. If I acknowledge it, he'll never shut up.

A ruckus rises in the street before me, some sort of confrontation between two men. I'm walking down it, my hands folded behind my back as they hold the basket of goods. I'd gone on a morning walk as I always do, the only time of day that truly gives me time to clear my head, but mostly, it had been a peaceful journey. I'd even ran into the Woozy in the forest, the strange creature usually far too shy to make its appearance. Though it lives in my domain, I've only seen the square creature a handful of times. Seeing it is usually a good sign, but I couldn't help but stare at the creature in sadness today. Some premonition told me it wouldn't always be so, that such creatures won't always walk free in Oz. With the worlds merging and new threats rising, nothing is as it seems anymore. A woozy today could be a World Breaker tomorrow.

The fight gets heated, the two men tumbling around each other as a ring of my subjects surround them to cheer them on. A female frantically yells at the men to stop it, possibly the source of the fight, but they continue tearing into each other. They all look at me as I walk by, as if to check if I'll stop it, but I don't care. If they want to fight over petty squabbles, they can do so. When they realize I'm not going to step in, the men hit harder. The smaller one catches the bigger one in the jaw and has him stumbling back, proof that it isn't always size that matter as much as technique.

I'm turning to go back to the castle, bored with the small-mindedness of my people, when something catches my nose's attention. A scent hits me, curls around my body as if in a tease. It's a predator, something larger than Oz should have but not larger than me. Still, the wild in the smell drags me to a stop, and I find myself turning to look up the street, waiting for the moment whatever it is appears.

For the first time in a long time, eagerness trickles into my soul.

CHAPTER THREE

FERAL

The scent drags me forward until I'm stumbling out of the thick trees into a street filled with creatures and people going about their daily lives. Where some of the places I've seen in this world were great technological magic, this street is not the same. I'm surprised to see the same yellow brick road cutting through the town that I'd followed through this world. Just like other sections, the part here is rust-stained, as if blood runs along it regularly. If I were less beast, I might have wondered whose sacrifice fed the cobblestones, but as it is, I barely pay mind to it passed the metallic undertones in the air. I only care about spilling my own prey's blood, not about that of someone else's kill.

As I break through the trees, the people before me on the messy road look up at the movement. Some of them barely react, creatures that have seen worse in the forest behind me, but the humans? Their eyes widen in horror, and they stumble backward. I'm a nightmare—I know I am—but it still stings something inside me to see such fear at my presence. It wasn't like that before. At least, I don't think so. The memories grow fuzzier every single day.

I take a step forward on furry wolven legs, my nose in the air to search for the scent that brought me here. It's stronger on the cobblestones, as if the scent is fresh. Whatever I'm tracking, whoever I search for, he's here. My teeth peel back over my lips in an excited growl. I've never smelled anything so. . .potent before. Anticipation at whatever I'll find hits me hard. A challenge. This will be a challenge.

Something tells me I used to love being challenged before I became Feral. I don't know how I know that or where the thought comes from, but something twists in my chest at the almost memory. Perhaps, it's not too late for me to remember who I was. Perhaps, I can be her again one day.

Someone screams as I move up the street and drags my attention to the left, distracting me from my hunt. Fury has me swiping out at the woman screaming, her great heaving bosom nearly spilling from her dress as she sucks in more air to scream again. Her skirts catch around her legs, tripping her up, and I can tell she thinks she's going to die as she falls uselessly to the ground. With as dangerous as the jungle is around here, I assumed everyone would have strong survival instincts here.

Apparently, I assumed wrong.

Without a doubt, this woman thinks she's going to die. She immediately descends into a sobbing mess of begging and prayers. I'm not sure who she prays to. I don't know the gods this world worships. Lucky for her, the scent fills my nose again and I'm tilting my head high to inhale it, my belly curling in excitement. Whatever he is, I want him. The beast I am purrs at the thought and I'm moving without care of the things I trample in my hast to find the monster. The small wagon filled with hay explodes as my legs slam through it, sending shards everywhere. Someone is yelling. People run around me chaotically, but I have one sole purpose.

Find him.

The air is tinged with fear and panic but baring my teeth at the creatures keeps them away for now. A few of them hold weapons pointed at me but they stay back. They're unsure of me, not quite understanding what sort of beast I am. I haven't killed anyone, not here, but I make a terrifying sight. I'm still covered in the blood of the square creature. The yellow coats my chin and chest where I hadn't thought to properly feed. Manners aren't something I worry about anymore. I'm a monster. Monsters feed like monsters.

A lizard-like creature attempts to stab me with a pitchfork as I pass. He gets within an inch of piercing my hide before my claws snap out and wrap around the handle, jerking him close because the foolish thing didn't think to release the pitchfork.

"Leave me alone," I snarl, my voice so thick with malice, he immediately lets go and falls on his ass. He scrambles backward along the dirt in his hast to put distance between us. His bravery is suddenly gone in the face of what I am.

An alarm sounds in the distance. I don't know if it's for me or something else, but my instinct says it's a warning for me. Someone is alerting the entire town of crudely built homes and the small castle in the distance. I pick up my pace. I don't know if he'll heed the warning or meet it head on, but I don't want to risk him getting away, not before I find him, not before I conquer him.

I round a corner of a thatched home, the yellow brick road suddenly curving to the left toward the castle spires I'd seen peeking over the homes. The scent wraps around me and kisses my fur, but I stumble to a stop.

There he is.

I expected a beast, but there, standing in the middle of the street, is a man.

Who I was before recognizes that he's beautiful. I can tell he's something astounding in beauty with the golden crown circling his head and his skin carved with scars where I can see it. Everything about him speaks of power and strength, but I also feel betrayed by his appearance. I wanted a challenge, a fight with a monster as large as I am.

The man tilts his head to the side as he studies me studying him. The people lining the street either watch in curiosity or rush inside their homes. I wonder if they know those makeshift shelters won't keep me out. I wonder if they know I could rip them to shreds.

He doesn't move. The man I'd hunted here simply stares at me from his place in the middle of the yellow brick road, his curiosity either making him foolish or confident. Either way, my instincts roar at me for the slight.

He's not the monster I am. He's just a man.

With a savage howl, I charge toward him.

CHAPTER FOUR

KING

I stare at the monstrous beast charging toward me in both interest and confusion. Something so hulking isn't from Oz. We have plenty of large creatures, but the larger a creature tends to be in Oz, the gentler they are, like the Woozy. The Woozy is large enough to cause damage, but it isn't capable of the actual destruction because of its nature. It's the smaller beasts you need to fear in Oz. This creature doesn't follow the rules of our world.

At first, I'd thought the creature causing chaos before sliding around the corner was Toto. It's been so long since I've seen him, I'd almost forgotten how he appeared. I was preparing myself to face off against a lobo coming to finish the job before two facts hit me at the same time. It takes me entirely too long to realize this beast is a different color altogether from Toto. It takes a few seconds longer to realize it's female.

Not Toto then, but still a threat.

This beast doesn't seem to wield magic. Though I can feel the buzz of it in the air, the beast never reaches for it, either out of ignorance or because it truly can't wield it, I don't know. Either way, I don't need to worry about such things. Clearly, this creature isn't going to use the magic that buzzes in the air around her. I'm not even sure it's hers.

She's salivating, feral in the way that creatures left too long in the dark are. Clearly, she has no calm instincts as she bolts toward me, closing the distance. My eyes trail down the yellow blood coating her fur. It's fresh, familiar, and when I realize why, my jaw clenches. I can't feel sorry for the Woozy that this creature clearly killed—I'm not capable of it anymore—but I can recognize the profoundness of such a gentle creature meeting its end. Long ago, I wondered how it had survived in a jungle meant to eat and kill. Finally, it fell at the hands of this beast, not even one of our own.

"You killed the Woozy," I comment, my brow raised. "How very cold of you."

A huff of fury escapes her even as she runs toward me, as if me pointing out her savagery offends her. She sees me as a challenge. She'd followed my scent here, had likely seen me as a threat, and though any other creature might back down, I'm an Heir.

If the monster wants to fight another monster, then so be it. It's been so long since I've faced the likes of her.

I drop the basket I'd been carrying, my contribution to the market my people stock. Lately, it has been filled with all sorts of new things with the worlds merging. The basket I have is full of fruit I've never seen before. When I drop it, it spills out over the road.

Crouching low and growling, I grin.

"Let's fight then, beast," I say.

She doesn't back down. If anything, the large wolf speeds up.

CHAPTER FIVE

FERAL

He doesn't seem afraid. Instead, the man goads me and then crouches down to meet my sprint. He takes up an offensive stance and waits for me. Somewhere in the back of my mind, a voice whispers that I should be letting him come to me if I want the advantage, but logic isn't something I utilize when my beast takes over. I can't control her, let along use reasoning to attack someone. Wisdom tells me I should attack in a way he won't see coming. Instinct tells me to go straight for the jugular and rip it out so he can bleed out beneath me.

I slam into him, expecting my momentum to send us rolling, but he's a brick wall. It nearly stuns me when I ram him and he doesn't move, my claws immediately trying to gain traction and make my mark. Laughter fills the air, husky, thick, masculine laughter that makes my insides dance again. What is this effect and why am I feeling it? I can't solve the puzzle right now, however. Not while I attempt to swipe my claws down his chest. He dances out of reach easily and I growl in frustration.

Angry, I swipe again, only to miss my target by a mile. The man is fast even in this form. Whatever monster he is, he doesn't show it to me. Instead, he wears his flesh as a badge of honor, mocking me. It's been so long since I've felt my flesh, I take it personally. How dare he rub it in my face? How dare he laugh at me as I attempt to tear him limb from limb?

Grinning, the man backs up a few steps so he can get a good look at me. I'm still for a moment, calculating, trying to find a weakness that I can't see. In this form, I'm taller than him, but still, it feels like I'm somehow looking up at him with the way he carries himself.

"Have you not been taught how to fight another beast, woman?" he asks suddenly, his head doing that infuriating tilt again, like I'm a creature to be studied for science. When I don't answer with anything other than a savage growl, he shakes his head. "How have you made it in the wild?"

White hot fury slams into me. Now he mocks me openly. Now he thinks I'm weak!

In a dazzling display of pure fury, I'm moving before I'm consciously aware of it. I want to hurt, to maim, to render him nothing but a pile of body parts in the middle of the yellow brick road. I want to wipe that smile from his face. My claws rake down the man's shoulder before he can dodge me, proving that I'm moving faster than even I realized. I should have never landed such a blow, not with how fast he is. The wound across his shoulder, though small in comparison to what I wanted to accomplish, surprises both of us. Not only am I looking at the three red lines in surprise, but so is he, as if he can't quite comprehend how they came to be there.

My lips curl up in an almost smile, pleased with myself. Those three marks are deep enough to scar and cause damage. He'll bear my mark for life even if I can't capture him to kill. Maybe I can land another blow.

But that thought goes out the window once I see the anger on his face. Oh, the big bad monster doesn't like it when someone lands a blow.

"What's the matter?" I ask, my voice thick with the wild. "Can't take a taste of your own medicine?"

I swipe out again, but it doesn't surprise me when I miss. It does, however, surprise me when the man moves faster than he had before, proving he'd been holding back out of pure curiosity. Before I know what's happened, my feet are swept out from beneath me and I'm slamming against the hard cobblestone on my back, my spine ricocheting with pain. I don't have time to get my feet back beneath me before he's on top of me, his teeth bared. Though he never shifts, his teeth are sharp and savage, menacing with threat simply by their appearance rather than any real effort.

"Stop it," he snarls in my face, spittle hitting my cheeks that would have made me cringe if I weren't more beast than human. "I've grown tired of this. Transform. Now."

I blink up at him and begin to fight his hold but he's stronger than he looks. Despite me being larger than him, he doesn't budge. His complete asshole attitude weighs more than he appears to.

"I said stop!" he snarls, claws digging into my arms as he holds me down. "Shift!"

But I don't remember who I was before. I don't know how to find her, don't know how to do what he asks. If I did, I would have done so long ago. When was the last time I sported flesh rather than fur? I can't even recall. Was it with Perry—

I snap at his face, but he stays out of range, wrapping clawed fingers around my neck to pin me better to the ground.

His brows raise before realization flashes in his eyes. "You can't shift back, can you?" he observes.

Struggling harder against his hold to no avail, I fall still for a moment, my eyes meeting his. I don't answer, don't admit to anything, but he sees my answer regardless.

With a grin, he pins my arms down with his knees, grinding into my bones in a way that almost hurts. "Not to worry, love. I'm curious enough that you're in luck."

He reaches inside his pocket and pulls out a tiny bottle of something. Before I can fight his hold again, he shakes something onto his hand and blows it in my face with a violence that makes my hackles rise.

Glitter dances in the air before me, dragging a sneeze forward I definitely don't want to feel with a full-grown man pinning me down.

The sneeze goes right into his face, but he doesn't seem to care. His eyes remain on me as he lets go and stands.

My ears start to ring. I sneeze again, sending the glitter in the air before me dancing. The people on the street rush into their homes when the man yells at them, but I'm only focused on the feeling of lightheadedness suddenly taking over. I drag myself to my feet, unsteady, but there's nothing for me to grab onto. What's happening? What has he done to me?

Pain slams into me a second later. White, hot fire fills my veins so suddenly, I double over in agony. A guttural scream peels form my lips as I fight the pain, as I desperately try to hold my insides where they belong. It feels like they're falling from my body, as if every organ will spill on this street and coat it.

A bone snaps and my back bows.

The howl that leaves my lips is nothing but pure, unadulterated pain.

CHAPTER

SIX

The shift is painful.

It's been so long since I last lost control and became the beast that I'd almost forgotten how painful it is for every single bone in your body to break at once. It feels like every organ in my body liquifies and reforms into their human counterparts. The fur I'd grown accustomed to sheds in bunches, dropping to the yellow brick beneath my cheek as I scream and scream and scream. My face cracks and concaves, the canine snout I'd lived with for. . .however long disappearing and reforming into a smaller human face. Brilliant red hair sprouts along my scalp and grows down my back, the waves tangling instantly with my thrashing.

I can't remember the last time I wore my flesh, so when soft peach skin replaces the fur, I almost don't recognize myself. I feel strange, as if I'm not at home in my own skin, as if this is no longer me. I'm a stranger in my own body, even as the beast recedes in my mind and my own consciousness takes over. The realization of what I am slams into me and I find myself curling into a tight ball as if that'll somehow stop the thoughts from getting in. Foolish, really. I've always been foolish.

As naked as a jaybird, I begin to shiver the moment I'm flesh and blood again, cold. I can't remember the last time I felt cold, too many winters ago. How long has it been? How long did the beast reign in my mind? How long had it been since Perry—

Realizing I'm still in the presence of a predator, one strong enough to somehow force my transformation and hold down my beast, I drag myself out of the wallowing and struggle to get my feet beneath me, but I'm weak from the change. My human limbs feel awkward and cumbersome. It takes me too long to stand on shaky legs, but I face off against the man, determined to not go down without a fight. I'm a woman. I'm naked in the street. I'm weak. I'm at a disadvantage, but at least all the townspeople are gone. A few curtains move from those peeking around the material but I've encountered worse situations than strangers seeing me naked. Nudity never scared me. I would have preferred to keep some modesty about myself in the face of this man though.

My hair is wild around me. I need to cut it. I don't remember it being this long but now I hangs down to my ass in a tangled mess. How long does it take for hair to grow so long? Can I even measure time in that way when I've been through various worlds?

The man's eyes trace down my dirty body, taking in my shape, before he looks up at me again. His lips move as he says something to himself, but it's so soft, I can't hear it. That alone tells me how quiet it is because I can hear the quiet mumble of the people inside their homes, can make out conversations. Apparently, though I'm no longer the beast, I still possess some of her powers.

On guard, I raise my brows at the man, unsure if we're still fighting or if I need to worry about something else altogether. Death isn't the worse thing a woman can face.

"You can't stay here," the man says suddenly, his tone harsh. I don't understand where the animosity suddenly comes from. At first, he'd seemed interested after my change. Now, he seems downright hostile. "Get out of my realm."

"And. . ." I clear my throat, attempting to get the roughness from it. I haven't used these vocal cords in too long. I'd barely used them when I'd been a wolf. It takes me a few precious seconds to feel confident enough to speak again. "And pray tell me, where am I supposed to go now?"

I don't even know what world I'm in now, what realm. I still can't decide if the man is a true threat or not. With a small gesture, I shrug my newly long hair over my shoulder, letting it cover as much as I'm able to. I'm still exposed, but it helps a little. The way the man is looking at me isn't helping matters. Nudity doesn't bother me, but apparently, standing nude before this man does.

"I won't make the same mistake," the man mutters to himself and I tilt my head, my brow crinkling. Who is he talking to? "Yes, but look at her."

"Who are you talking to?" I ask, frowning. I glance around, as if I've missed someone else but we're the only two on the street. He doesn't answer me. Instead, he simply stares into my eyes, consciously not looking down as if he's afraid to see me naked. That, or he's simply being respectful now.

"No one."

"I heard you," I point out.

"Mind your fucking business," he growls and turns to walk toward the caste.

"That's it?" I ask, putting my hands on my hips. Though I'm weak, I can't help the attitude at the situation.

My mother used to chastise me for my boldness.

Surprise at the sudden memory of her whacking me with a rolled newspaper after a smart remark passing my brain makes me straighten. I hadn't been able to remember my name before but suddenly, things come slamming back as if waiting for me to acknowledge them.

When he doesn't answer, I take a step after him. "You blow some dust in my face and force me to change back and then leave me naked in the street?"

He pauses with his back to me, his shoulders tense. "I helped you."

"And what should I do when I change again, and I'm trapped as the beast for another year?" I don't mean for my voice to shake, don't mean for the words to be choked out, but I can't really control them. Later, I'll chalk it up to the weakness of the transformation, but right now, I know it for what it is.

Fear.

If possible, his shoulder tense more, and then he's looking over his shoulder at me. "A year?"

I cringe at the sudden realization that I don't even know. "It could have been longer," I admit. "It was. . .difficult to keep time."

For a moment, he doesn't move, and I think about how cold he looks. There's no empathy on his face, nothing to give me any reassurance of traction. He looks like he'll happily leave me in the street nude, content with his soul to leave me helpless and weak at the mercy of his realm, but just when I think he's going to walk away, he turns to me and grabs the hem of his shirt. With a quick, masculine jerk, he pulls it smoothly over his head.

He tosses it to me without hesitation, an olive branch or a manipulation, I can't tell, but I still shrug it on. The scent of him, the same scent that had dragged my wolf to him, envelopes me, and I'm ashamed of how aroused it makes me. If I can smell that arousal, he certainly can with whatever beast he carries inside him, but he doesn't comment on it. If I'm lucky, he doesn't notice.

"Perhaps, you should come with me until I figure out what to do with you." He sighs. "I can't allow some half-controlled beast to tear through my realm. You already killed the woozy."

"The Woozy?" I whisper, an image of the square creature popping into my mind. "I didn't mean to."

"Yes, well, you've killed possibly one of the only genuinely good creatures in Oz for a meal. The rest of us. . ." He studies the way the hem of the shirt drops to my thighs and seems to nod in satisfaction that I'm covered up. "Well, we aren't so good."

I tense, guilt hitting me about killing the poor creature, but it can't really be helped now. It's on the tip of my tongue to apologize, but something tells me this man, whoever he is, wouldn't care for it. It's been done. I'd stained my soul with the woozy. I add it to my mental list of those I've killed, a list that has grown far too long. At the top, right at the beginning, is—

"Come on, woman," he orders, and begins walking to the castle again.

My instincts tell me to fight him ordering me around like a dog, but

I realize logically he's my best bet of figuring out where I am and what I should do.

With a huff of annoyance, I pick my way across the cobblestone and follow him into the castle.

CHAPTER SEVEN

KING

I stare at the woman sitting across from me at the long table I'd had set up for two. She's currently tearing her way through mostly raw meat, pieces of it sticking to her chin as she rips it apart with dull human teeth. Even in her flesh, she's savage, her beast within just under the surface. Her control of herself is non-existent, and though I don't care for her plight one way or the other, I can't let her roam around my realm to kill my people. If I'm to have a realm, I need people to rule over, and it's my job to keep them mostly alive. At least from outside forces. And this woman, she's certainly an outside force.

She's hardly looked at me since the meat had been brought out. Only when she'd begun tearing into it hungrily had I realized how truly skinny she is. Clearly, she's been hunting, if the tang of the Woozy's blood on her gives me any hints, but perhaps, she hasn't been hunting enough. If she can't control herself, she might hardly know how to hunt properly in her wolf form. No wonder she'd gone after the gentle woozy.

"Poor thing. We should help her," a soft voice says in my mind.

"Too risky," I mumble under my breath. The woman looks up at me but doesn't say anything. Instead, she continues to eat, filling herself with so much food, she's going to make herself sick. Still, I don't stop her. I understand what it's like to be hungry too well.

"*If she keeps eating like that, she's going to make herself sick,*" the soft voice echoes my thoughts.

"*You know the risk of keeping a woman here,*" another voice growls, all gravel.

I ignore both voices and instead focus on the woman.

"Where did you come from?" I ask aloud, speaking loud enough to both be heard across the long table and drown out the bickering voices.

She looks up from the fowl leg she'd been pulling meat from. A bit of red drips down her chin at her pause and she wipes it away with the back of her arm. Manners are lost on her, either because she's never been taught or because she'd been as her wolf too long. When she glances down at her arm in dismay, I bet on the later. She was properly trained. She'd just been wild for too long and has fallen out of habit.

I can see her mind turning at my question, but she doesn't answer right away. It's almost like she doesn't remember the answer and she has to sift through her mind to find it.

"*She's been a beast for longer than a year,*" the softer voice says. "*She can't even remember her home.*"

After too long, she finally sighs and meets my eyes. Though it took her minutes to find the answer, she's certain when she says, "Home was the Grimm Forest."

I tilt my head in curiosity. "And how did you find yourself in Oz?"

"Oz," she repeats softly, tasting the word, before she shrugs. "I don't remember how I got here. I don't remember leaving Grimm."

"The worlds are merging," I offer as an answer, magnanimous. Perhaps, if I show her we can be mutually beneficial, I can better figure out what to do with her. If she trusts me, it'll be easier to control her. "Your world probably merged with mine briefly enough for you to cross over and disappeared. They seem to be moving chaotically around the realm. The Grimm Forest is also currently merged with Gillikin City, another quadrant of Oz." I narrow my eyes. "Your name?"

She hesitates, wondering if she should give me such an important piece of information, but eventually, she speaks around the leg held against her lips. "I go by 'Red', but my birth name is Scarlett."

Nodding, I take in the red hair framing her face. "It fits. You can call me King."

She doesn't answer. Instead, she eyes me suspiciously and continues to eat. I shrug at her aloofness and instead, reach for the last leg on the platter in the middle of the table. Before I can wrap my hand around the bone, she slams a large claw down through the meat of it with a snarl and drags it across the table to her. Her face is savage as she picks it up and tears into it, a threat in her eyes as she looks over the leg at me, daring me to react. Instead, I find myself smirking.

"*We should send her on her way,*" the gravel voice commands.

"Yes," I hum softly, quiet enough that I can't be heard over the sounds of ripping meat. "But think of the fun we can have with her."

The soft voice snorts in my mind. "*That creature will rip you to shreds if you turn your back on her.*"

My lips stretch into a smile.

"I know."

CHAPTER EIGHT

JUPITER

S itting in the dark bedroom I share with White, I stare at my fingers. White is off with Tin discussing the worlds he knows, and the first moment I'd been able to, I'd escaped on my own. I had to.

By nature, I'm a social creature. Most humans are. I like being around the people I care about, even if I need a long time to recharge, but lately, I'm starting to need more and more alone time, if only so I can try to solve the problem I'm currently having.

As I stare at my fingers, tiny glittering sparks dance around the tips, magical, enthralling, and completely foreign. I've never been able to manifest power like this before and my shield magic is failing because I keep trying to control it how I had before. I haven't figured out much about the power except for it doesn't like to be controlled the same way as I had once utilized it. The longer we're in Oz, the more things are starting to not make any sense. My body buzzes with power. Things are changing and I can't control it.

I feel. . .chaotic. . .and powerful.

I absentmindedly swirl my fingers in the air and the sparks dance around my fingertips like a caress, brushing against my skin with tiny zaps that make something unfurl in my chest I can't figure out. Is it my mercy powers? The Dreamwalker ones? But no. I haven't been dreaming lately. This feels like something else, something. . .dangerous.

There's a soft one, two, three knock on the door and the sparks fizzle out just in time for Clara to push the door open and peek her head in. She frowns when she sees me sitting in the dark on the edge of the bed. It takes everything in me to school the guilt, so it doesn't appear on my face. Clara and Cal are my friends, so close they might as well be sisters, and here I am, hiding something so large from them. But I'm afraid. I'm afraid of what I'm becoming. I'm afraid they'll look at me different if I tell them.

"You okay?" Clara asks, pushing inside the rest of the way. The door swings wide to reveal her large pregnant belly. She's due any day now. I've done my best to take care of her throughout her pregnancy but I'm not a labor doctor. Somehow, I'm still one of the few qualified to even check her. Wonderland hasn't had babies in an awfully long time, and no one seems to remember anyone who was a midwife that had survived the Red Queen. Briella Mae admitted she'd helped birth a calf once but had no experience with people. Oz doesn't have children. The only other person who has been able to help is Tiger Lily since she'd given birth herself. Back in Wonderland, Old Mother could have helped, but she hadn't come with us to Oz. It's up to Tiger and me to help Clara along. The pressure. . .well, I'm not handling that pressure well, either.

Not wanting her to worry about me when she has enough to worry about, I smile brightly at Clara. Though we're close, she's exhausted and doesn't realize my smile doesn't reach my eyes. "Just came to clear my head. The puzzle of all these worlds merging and flashing around like portals is still confusing me."

Clara smiles gently. "I'm the same," she admits. "All this madness and no explanation." Her hands rub her large belly, and my eyes drop to it. Somehow, I can feel the power of the baby inside her and I wonder when that ability started. I can feel magic where I hadn't before. "You'll figure it out though," Clara continues. "You're so smart. I have full faith in you."

But my mind is on the baby now and the power I can feel around Clara. I can feel the power sing.

I gesture to her belly. "Do you think he'll be like you, or the Hatter?" I ask suddenly, my mind filling in the blanks. I don't realize my mistake until Clara freezes, her eyes jerking up to mine.

"What do you mean 'he'?" she asks.

My body goes still, the power in my own veins humming loudly in my ears until they gently ring. "Oh, I don't know, of course," I hurry to explain. "I just. . .had a feeling."

Clara studies me for a few long tense seconds before she shakes her head and glances down at her belly. A tiny smile pulls at her lips. "I don't know how the baby will be. I'm just hoping for healthy."

I smile, relieved that she hadn't pursued the comment. In these worlds, we don't have ultrasounds so there's no way to know if the baby is a boy or a girl. I don't know why the baby feels like a boy to me, but the more I focus on the energy, the more I'm certain of my statement. I shouldn't be able to tell, shouldn't know, but I hide the knowledge away in my mind.

"Of course. I'll be here to help any way I'm able when the time comes to welcome the baby into the world," I say, smiling brightly again. This time, I know I'm not as convincing, but I can't help it. I'm suddenly desperate to get away from someone far too clever. Eventually, Clara will see through me and know something is wrong. I don't want her to worry, not in her state. Standing and stretching my arms, I add, "I'm going to go find White. He should be done talking to Tin by now."

"Don't go too far," Clara says, taking the hand I offer to help her up off the bed. She's carrying forward, all belly, making her waddle in the cutest way, but I know Hatter will go after anyone who lets her strain. Unfortunately for him, Clara is just as stubborn and insists on doing whatever she wants. I don't envy him. He's probably looking for his mate frantically right now upon realizing he can't see her.

"Are there more banshees?" I ask, my brows furrowing.

"Not that I've heard, no. But Tin said he saw Hansel and Gretel sneaking around again. They're scheming and I wouldn't want you caught up in it."

Nodding, I hold the door open for the empress and wait until she waddles through before I close the door behind me on the tiny sparks attempting to follow in my wake. They don't come through the door.

"I won't go too far," I promise. "Take care that you're resting. Tiger says you'll start feeling more exhausted soon."

"I'm already there," Clara admits, brushing her hair out of her face. "But I'll be fine. I'll let you know if anything changes."

I smile again and nod, before waving and turning to walk away. I can feel Clara's eyes on me all the way down the hallway. Only when I turn the corner is the connection broken and I'm able to breath out a puff of air.

Once outside, I glance around for White but don't see him. The forest is still growing through Gillikin city. It's strictly off limits with creatures like banshees coming out of it often, but something inside me whispers to step into the tree line, to venture into the darkness. The Grimm Forest beckons me, and I find myself a single step inside it, staring off into whatever lays in the distance.

Tiny, tiny sparks flicker around me in the air, winking like the fires of time.

In the distance, something growls in warning, but I don't know if it's warning me away, or warning me to follow. . .

CHAPTER NINE

RED

The bed is tousled after our earlier love making, the sheets ripped loose, the pillows scattered on the floor. We'd fallen into a contented sleep only to wake up hours later to the early morning sounds of people preparing for the day. The walls are paper thin, letting in all the sounds of the neighbors tossing out their water and arguing between themselves even if those sounds are slightly muted. It's enough to wake me from my slumber, to have me yawning and stretching in Perry's arms.

Perry is sweet enough, the best man in the village as far as I'm concerned. He hardly drinks so I never have to worry about him coming home and beating me in a drunken stupor like my father used to do my mother. He's a blacksmith, so he makes decent money and he's very hardworking. Passed all that, he's simply a kind man. The young boy I'd grown up with in this village had grown to be a proper gentleman and I know how lucky I am that he's chosen me as his girl-friend over the other twittering females of the village.

I lay there for a few moments, cuddled against Perry's naked chest, my fingers stroking through the light smattering of hair along his pectorals as if I'm petting him. It's a favorite pastime, just enveloped

36

within each other's arms, but though I care for Perry, though I know he loves me, I still don't know if I genuinely love him. How does one measure such intense emotion? Is it butterflies? Is it a fear of losing that person? I have none of that. Perry is a great man, but he isn't unique. He makes me feel comfortable, certainly, but butterflies? Sparks?

"What are you thinking about, Scarlett?" Perry's deep voice interrupts my thinking. He always does that, calling me Scarlett rather than 'Red'. The only other person who calls me by my full name is my mother and even then, she only does it when she's preparing to chastise me.

"Nothing," I whisper too quickly, my finger starting to trace the lines of the star tattoo embedded in Perry's skin. It dances along his collarbone, temptation. I remember when he got it, how the village girls cooed over the art. It's pretty enough, but I'm not with Perry because of his tattoo. I'm with him because he's a desirable choice among so many bad ones. Even my mother can't argue with the choice. Hell, sometimes, I think she prefers Perry to her own daughter.

Perry hums in a way that I feel deep in his chest where my ear presses against him. "You always were stuck with your head in the clouds."

Words he's always told me, even when we were children. I'm known as the dreamer, the girl with her mind so far away you can't reach her. According to the other villagers, it's almost charity work for Perry to be with me. The bastards think I'm useless.

"Better my head in the clouds than my feet on the ground to rot," I shoot back.

The rumble surprises me. Where my ear lays against Perry's chest, I feel the growl more than I can hear it. Perry never growls at me. He's always so good-natured. Confused, I slowly lift up onto my elbows and look up at the man who has been a rock in my life for years. I stare at him, at the sudden changes.

Outside, the arguing of the neighbors gets louder before fading into static.

"Perry," I mutter, staring at him. "What big eyes you have."

Those eyes glow even in the early morning light. Perry's eyes are blue normally, but right now, they look almost golden, like an animal in the early morning hours stalking its prey.

"The better to see you with, Scarlett," he replies, blinking at me. His chest continues to rumble with the growl. His lips part in a smile that feels more like he's baring the suddenly large canines at me.

Gasping, I sit up further. "Perry, what big teeth you have."

The grin widens. The next time he speaks, his voice is thick and no longer his own. Gone is the kind man I'd agreed to be with. Gone is the man who gives me comfort.

"The better to eat you with, little Scarlett."

My heart stops just before Perry opens his wide mouth and snaps at me, those impossibly large teeth aiming right for my jugular.

I COME TO SO VIOLENTLY, I THROW MYSELF FROM THE BED I'D collapsed on the night before, landing on the dirty floor with a thump that sends a cloud of dust flying around me. Covered in a cold sweat, the dust settles on my skin and sticks to me, forcing an equally violent sneeze from my nose. I'm panting hard, sucking in more of the dust in way that has it coating my throat thickly, making me gag on it. My stomach revolts against the sudden vision of Perry again, making me dry heave and shake on the floor, but nothing comes up. Nothing ever does, not anymore.

Dragging myself to shaking feet and shoving my too long hair out of my eyes, I look down at the bed I'd thrown myself on after the meal last night. I'd had a full belly after a long stint of barely eating enough to survive, so I'd been barely coherent afterwards, exhaustion dragging at my limbs until I'd collapsed without care. The sheets where I'd laid are shredded beyond repair, my claws having done a number on them while I'd suffered through the nightmare. There will be no stitching them back together and I frown in embarrassment. I'll have to tell King what I'd done or suffer shredded sheets the entire time. Likely, I'll choose to simply suffer rather than inform him of the mess I've made. Maybe I can find some replacements before he sees it.

The room hadn't been cleaned before I'd been offered it. Clearly.

Not only is the floor and furniture covered with a thick layer of dust, but so is the bed. I'd fallen asleep in the dust. I can't say that was any good for my lungs, but it can't be worse than the thick, suffocating smoke of a burning village. Unfortunately for me, I have plenty to compare it to.

Studying the room closer, I realize it hasn't been used in a long time. Either King doesn't typically have guests, or he'd given me a room never used. Either way, I'm still grateful he'd offered at all. He could have left me on the street nude with nowhere to go. I'm not foolish enough to think he's allowed me to stay for any other reason than he's interested in where I came from, but I'm still grateful regardless.

Sighing at the state of the bed, I drag the tattered sheets from the mattress and move into the equally dusty bathroom to relieve myself before ripping strips free and wetting them. They're already ruined so I might as well finish the job. Then, because I can at least show my appreciation, I begin to clean the dust from every surface of the room. Without a broom, I can't do much more than dirty each strip of the sheet. I'll clean myself up once the room is clean enough, I won't have to worry about dust sticking to my skin anymore. As it is right now, I'll only get dirty again, so I settle myself with cleaning my face briefly in between clearing the dust from the room and picking up forgotten items.

I don't know how long King will allow me to stay in his castle. I assume not long at all. At least until he deems me no threat to his realm.

The problem is that I'm very much the threat he thinks I am.

The beast I carry inside me is in no way leashed. If anything, I feel as if it's me who wears the leash, always at the whims of the monster in my veins. I'd taken to calling her Feral at the beginning, naming her as if she's simply a parasite that I need to be rid of. There's no cure for the ailment I have—that I know anyways—but there'd once been a time where I'd hoped there was. That hope has long since disappeared. If there was hope, I wouldn't be Feral.

Still, I don't know anything about King. He could be keeping me here with plans to hurt me. He could be planning to cage me for the rest of my life. But despite the lack of knowledge and his strange mumbling to himself, King seems the safest place for me right now. Somehow, he'd forced me back to flesh after too long being at the mercy of Feral. I feel safe here, if only because I know King can force me back to human no matter how much control Feral has over my body.

I'm slowly finishing up cleaning the wardrobe when I turn to grab another strip of sheet. My eyes catch on a pair of glowing eyes in the corner, and suddenly, I'm right back in the nightmare.

Before I can do anything to stop it, the first bone pops and Feral dances at the edge of my consciousness.

CHAPTER

TEN

"Stop your change," King growls as he steps from the shadows. Not Perry. Just a grumpy king with a penchant for being an asshole. Not Perry. Not Perry. *Not Perry.*

Another bone pops and I grunt in agony, clutching at my skin in an attempt to stop the change. I'm finally in my flesh again. I don't want to give up control to Feral so soon. My femur snaps and reforms, but only on one leg, leaving me standing crooked and barely holding myself up against the wardrobe I'm suddenly in desperate need of to keep standing.

"I said, 'stop it'," King growls again, advancing on me.

"I can't," I admit with a grunt, trying my hardest to push back Feral. Another bone pops, bowing me backwards, and I scream at the torture. My teeth grind together as I push as hard as I can against Feral in my mind, as I shove backward and refuse to budge, but just like me, Feral is stubborn, and she wants free.

Another bone pops in my leg and I collapse to the ground. My face fights between the wolf features and my own, lengthening and shrinking in a painful dance.

"You can't control your change because you fear it," King says, watching closely as he begins to circle my writhing body. "Accept your beast and become one."

Revulsion has me shaking my head despite the pain. I'm keeping Feral at bay but just barely. Only by pure will am I holding her back. If she gains even a hint of an upper hand, it's done for. I'll be ripping through the castle in no time.

"I'm no beast," I snarl at him, but my voice comes out garbled with the fight between wolf and woman. My face shrinks again as I lift myself on shaking hands. My wrist pops and I nearly collapse again, but before I can, clawed fingers wrap around my throat and lift me until I'm pinned against the wall. I can't even fight against him without losing control of the change. I'm barely holding her back. Still, my fingers wrap around his wrist, my own claws digging into his skin. Though I draw blood, he hardly seems to notice.

"Yes," he replies, his voice calm and steady. "You are."

I scream in absolute agony, determined to show I'm no monster. I refuse to allow Feral to become me, refuse to become a slave to instinct and bloodlust. I want to remain in my flesh, want to continue to grow acclimated to my own body again, and I can't do that if I'm Feral. I shove so hard against the change, a fine sheen of sweat breaks out on my forehead. I writhe in King's hold, forcing bones back to their original shape, fighting against everything fluctuating through me. It takes so much of my strength, I know I'll be useless after this, but I refuse to be the wolf again so soon.

Tears leak from the corner of my eyes and King watches them fall, no emotion on his face, as if the sight of my pain and struggle leave him completely unmoved. With pure strength of will, I push against the instinct to change triggered by the sight of golden eyes. I can't even trust my dreams anymore when they bleed into my waking hours.

My insides feel as if they liquify and reform, split in half and mend back together. Every nerve ending is shrieking at me as Feral finally retreats into my mind, not completely gone but relinquishing control of my body back to me. The final bones pop back into place, my claws retreat, and my body slumps in King's hold.

"You're weak," King finally says, studying me. "You can't even control something that's an integral part of you."

"The beast I carry isn't me," I argue, my voice soft with the weakness he accuses me of, yet I can't bring myself to care. I don't have the energy to care.

He tilts his head. "It is now. It's better to accept it."

"Or what?" I ask, panting. Stopping the change has taken too much of me. The last pains of the change disappear, leaving my tingling flesh as it should be. Exhaustion grabs at me, the power it took to stop the change so vast, I can't fight King if I wanted to.

"Or it's best to put you out of your misery," he states, no emotion in those words either, as if he regularly threatened to kill people. Who knows? Perhaps he does. He's powerful, after all.

Finally, his claws release me, and I nearly collapse because he'd given me no warning. Somehow, I don't think he'll care if I collapse where I stand and stay there. Clearly, the king has no feelings at all. I just barely catch myself on the wardrobe again, keeping on my feet out of sheer stubbornness.

"You going to be the one who pulls the trigger?" I ask, my voice harder than I intend.

He looks at me for a moment, as if searching for something. I don't know what he finds, but he eventually shrugs and says, "yes. All beasts must know their end." He glances at the rest of the half-cleaned room, taking in the shredded sheets and the dust. "I'll have someone finish this later."

Then he turns and walks toward the door I'd never even heard him open to get inside. I watch as he leaves, and only when I'm certain he's gone do I release my hold on the wardrobe and collapse to my knees.

I curl up right there in the dust and fall asleep before I know what I'm doing, too exhausted to even close my mouth against the dirt coating my throat.

CHAPTER ELEVEN

I don't wake up again until a day later, my body so drained, it keeps me in statis until it deems me strong enough to move again. When I wake, I find myself not where I'd collapsed, but on clean sheets in the plush bed. In fact, the entire room is clean as if there'd never been a drop of dust. I don't know if King had come in and put me in the bed or someone else did, but I'm grateful for whoever took care of me.

Taking stock of my body before I move, I realize I don't hurt. Either I'd truly slept off the exhaustion or Feral had decided not to punish me for refusing the change. Sometimes, she's so angry, my bones will ache for days after, until I beg her to change and remove the horror of it. This time, I'm free of even a single ache.

"Thank you, Feral," I breathe softly. My chest warms in answer, an acknowledgement. She doesn't try to force a change again, simply settles in my mind. I can feel her anxiousness though, so I carefully climb from the bed and clean myself up. Taking my long hair in my fingers, I quickly braid it just as my mother showed me as a child, getting it out of my face and out of my way. I'll need to cut it soon to avoid it getting any longer, but that can wait. For now, I need to settle Feral's anxiousness or I'm going to end up fighting her every hour of the day.

That's how I find myself outside an hour later, sitting in the shorter grass. I keep my distance from any plant life that moves, far from the trees that line the back of the castle, but there's a nice enough garden. Though overgrown, there's still a section that's been tended to enough to sit and meditate. With my legs crossed and my eyes closed, I sit out there and focus on my breathing.

Breathe in, one, two, three. Breathe out, one, two, three. Repeat.

Feral settles inside me and quiets, curled into a ball like a puppy with a full belly. When she sleeps like this, it's almost easy to forget she's there, almost easy to forget what I become when she takes control. Though she's there, though I don't want to change, I know Feral isn't evil. I know she's simply a beast of instinct and nothing more, but still, my mind revolts against the thought of accepting her. I'm human, not a monster. I don't want to be a monster.

"You need to control it." King's voice breaks through my hard-earned silence and stirs the wolf.

Scowling, I don't open my eyes to see King standing over me. I don't need to know what he looks like. My mind provides a perfectly clear picture that Feral sits up and pays attention to.

"Fuck off," I tell him without looking at him. I'm sure it pisses him off, but I hardly care. He's interrupting my silence.

"You'll either kill yourself or someone else," he continues.

I shrug, annoyed. "I already have," I admit, and despite my best efforts, images of those I've killed start to flash across my mind. I remember each and every one, down to the Woozy I'd killed just before coming here. "It's nothing new to have blood under my nails." In fact, before I'd become Feral, I was still used to that feeling. Life isn't always a pretty thing.

"What are you even doing?" he asks, and I can feel his condescension. "Gods won't help you."

"I'm not praying," I grunt, my nose wrinkling at him despite not seeing him. "Gods are nothing more than the meek hope someone will save you. There's no help from a genie in the sky. I'm meditating."

I can literally feel his distaste when he says, "and this helps?"

"When it's fucking silent it does," I growl, opening my eyes finally to look up at the idiot with a scowl. "Look, I realize you

45

think I need to control the beast inside me, but I like making her sleep."

Seeing him standing over me does something to my core I'm not proud of. Though I know it for the bad idea it is, though I refuse to give into my wild, I can't help but admire the man. He's gorgeous, far prettier than any man who'd lived in my village. Someone like him would have had his pick of the women and he certainly wouldn't have given me, the troublesome town redhead, a second look. My treacherous body doesn't seem to care, however. She likes what she sees, and it doesn't help that Feral sits up at attention just the same. Traitors.

"Which is why your beast is controlled by your emotions rather than your will," he points out.

I sigh. "And what do you know? You keep speaking as if you know what's it's like to have an actual beast inside you and yet you're nothing more than a man with claws."

The grin that splits his lips holds his secrets and I know before he speaks that I'm wrong, that he does have something inside of him he chooses not to show. "What makes you think I don't have my own beast?"

Studying him, I narrow my eyes. "You're no wolf."

"I never said I was," he shrugs. Then, under his breathe, he mutters something I can't hear despite my advanced hearing.

"What?"

But he shakes his head. "I came out here to tell you to leave, however, perhaps we can make a deal instead."

I narrow my eyes in suspicion. "What sort of deal?"

He lords over me as if he's used to being a king. I suppose he is, but still, it irks me. Even if I stand, I'll be looking up to the bastard. I should start carrying around a ladder so at any time, I can be taller than him. Wouldn't that be something?

"You teach me meditation," he says, his face smug. "And in return, I'll teach you how to not fear your she-wolf."

I unfold my legs and stand, my face hard. "I'm not afraid," I deny.

He only raises his brow at me, tasting the lie. "You're so afraid, woman, I can taste your fear." He sniffs and wrinkles his nose. I only hope fear is all he smells. "Follow me."

I'm scowling at his back as he walks away, expecting me to follow like a dog, but after some intense cursing of him toward his back, I move to follow him.

After all, I'm curious enough to see if he can really do what he promises.

CHAPTER TWELVE

I stare at the walls of the large, caged dungeon, the metal bars threatening in their surrounding of me. I'd followed King through the castle and down until he'd finally led me to this damp dungeon. It clearly hasn't been used in a long time just like my room, but beneath the scent of rot and decay, I can smell old blood. It isn't being used now, but some time ago, it was used for precisely what it was intended for.

I glance back at King as he closes the door, not only shutting me inside, but himself.

"Is this where you lock me away and throw away the key?" I ask, raising my brow.

Despite the very real threat that King could choose to do that, I'm not afraid. It would almost be a relief to be locked away until I can control Feral.

King snorts. "If I were smart, that's exactly what I'd do." He pauses, as if he's listening to something. "Shut up."

Tilting my head, I frown at the man. "I didn't say anything."

He shakes his head at me, as if to say he wasn't talking to me, but then, who was he talking to?

Deciding to face it head on rather than continuing to ignore it, I cross my arms and face him.

"Why do you talk to yourself so much? Are you crazy?"

My words make King freeze. For someone who barely shows emotion, he doesn't actually have a great poker face when dealing with a question he doesn't want to answer.

"I don't talk to myself," he denies, looking away. Suddenly, the walls are incredibly interesting to him.

"You do it all the time," I argue. "Constantly."

A low growl echoes in the room. "You don't know what you're talking about. Who's to say you're not the crazy one?"

I scoff. "All a large number of words to convince me you're not clearly talking to someone in your mind. Why so defensive if there's nothing wrong with you?" I goad. I know I'm pushing at his buttons, but if I'm going to trust him to show me how to control my wolf, I'd like to know exactly what I'm getting myself into.

King's face changes and this time, when he looks me in the eyes, he doesn't feel the same. That thought only grows stronger when he speaks. His voice is different, deeper, harsher. "There's nothing wrong with us!" he snarls.

I don't take a step back though that would have been my instinct before I became a predator myself. He's menacing, a walking threat, and it would be smart not to antagonize him. Still, the attitude doesn't leave my voice. I can't help it. I'm still my mother's daughter.

"Whatever you say." I hold up my hands in mock surrender and it only makes him scowl harder.

"Let's get on with it," he growls, and his voice is normal again, as if he'd been someone completely different a few seconds ago.

Instead of pushing, I file it away for later, vowing to keep a close eye on him. He's clearly lying about it—I've heard him too many times talking to himself and answering silence—but I can't do anything about it now. I'd just like to make sure and know if I'm staying with someone crazy rather than finding out when he tries to slaughter me in my sleep later.

"Your beast is as much a part of you as breathing," King says, continuing forward as if we hadn't just had a conversation about my very real accusation. "By singing her to sleep, it makes her prone to your emotions, as much a slave to them as you are. She's at the whim of them. By learning to control her and accepting her, you will allow her to learn when it's ideal to sleep and when it's ideal to wake."

I breathe deep, releasing the air in a quick release. "What if I don't want her to be awake?"

"If you merge with her, you don't have to change. You'll be able to tell her when she can take over and she'll listen."

I crack my knuckles. "Okay. So tell me what to do."

King moves in a circle around me, studying me as I roll my shoulders. "Accept her."

Scoffing, I turn to meet his eyes as he stalks behind me. "You've said that. *How* do I accept her?"

He shrugs. "How is up to you. Talk to her. Reach out and stroke your finger down her consciousness. I don't know what it takes to merge with your beast."

"Great," I groan. Rolling my shoulders again, I close my eyes, picturing Feral. "Hey, Feral," I say out loud, talking to her. "I need to accept you and for you to accept me. Think we can do that?"

King pauses. I know because I hear him stop in front of me. "You named your wolf?"

"Of course. I needed something to call her."

"Then call her by your name. She's you."

I tense, but instead of arguing the point, I keep focusing on Feral where she's curled up in my consciousness. I don't know how to talk to her, but because she's a canine, the only thing I can think to do is mentally reach out with my hand and wait for her to smell me. A dog, when it accepts you, will allow you to pet it. Perhaps, Feral is as simple as that.

"Come here, girl," I coax, and though I'm talking to the beast in my mind, it feels better to speak aloud. I don't know if she's going to think I'm an asshole for talking to her this way, but it's the best I can think to do. "I'm not going to hurt you."

I feel her uncurl in my mind, picture her doing just that. Strangely, I can almost feel her stretch which is a weird thing to think about. Is it my mind stretching? Am I imagining her being so physical?

King continues in a circle around me, watching, waiting, as I encourage the wolf forward to smell my hand. I feel the danger as she comes closer, and before I can stop it, a bone snaps in my arm. I grunt in pain, but don't drop my hand I have outstretched toward her in my mind.

"Don't let her take control. Accept her. Don't fear her," King orders.

"I'm trying," I grit, attempting to ignore when a bone in my hand pops. I don't even cry out in pain for that one in the hopes that I won't spook her into taking over.

The wolf inside me gets close enough that her nose tickles against me. Though it's all in my mind, I still feel whiskers dance over the palm of my hand. Another snap has me tilting sideways.

"Release your fear, Red," King growls. "You're holding onto your fear."

When Feral presses her nose against my hand, scenes flash in front of my eyes, gory scenes from where I'd ripped through people when she was in charge. Regret hits me, guilt, pain. I've killed so many. Feral has killed so many.

Though I try my hardest to push the images away, I can't. I see each victim, hear them scream out in agony as I tore through their soft bodies. I can't. I can't.

"I can't," I breathe shakily. My body begins to tremble. Another large bone pops.

In my mind, Feral's lips curl up at the fear that permeates the air. She looks up at me, and despite her annoyance, her eyes are sad. She wants me to accept her, wants me to get there, but instead, here I am afraid. I'm afraid of her and what she turns me into. I'm afraid of the massacre I'll leave in my wake.

"I'm sorry," I croak, just before Feral snaps out and latches around my hand. Pain ricochets up my arm despite her not really biting me. The bones begin popping faster and all control I'd attempted to gain vanishes as if it had never been there. I collapse to the ground and writhe in pain as my bones break and lengthen, as things rearrange themselves in my body and I shred through the shirt King had given me before.

To King's credit, he doesn't run and leave me in the cage alone. He stands against the wall to give me room to shift, and when I stand, a great hulking wolf, he doesn't back down. Instead, he meets my eyes, and I can feel his disappointment so clearly, it splits the air.

CHAPTER THIRTEEN

KING

"Control her," I order harshly, watching the werewolf carefully. As a wolf, she's a magnificent beast. Taller than I am in my human form, she stands tall enough to intimidate anyone. I don't know how she became the wolf, but whoever turned her was a strong bloodline. Werewolves aren't always so large, aren't always so strong. Despite her not accepting the wolf, Red is still strong enough to hold it at bay. The last time, she'd stopped the change though it had taken everything inside her. When I'd went back in hours later to find her passed out on the floor, I'd carefully put her in the bed, not because I care, but because it's best to rest in comfort in times like those. If I want to work with her, it's best she keeps herself in her prime.

The wolf shakes her head at my words, and though she's transformed, I can still see Red's consciousness in her eyes.

"You're allowing her to run the show when it should be you. Control her."

"I can't," she grunts, and though I'm facing off against the wolf, the wolf is all Red. It's as if she swallowed gravel, but her awareness is in those words. Red is still attempting to gain control. Progress, but she doesn't know it and I won't tell her. She'll have so much further to go if she wants to truly control herself.

"You're letting your fear get in the way," I point out, folding my hands behind my back.

"I'm not afraid," she replies, but we both hear the lie in those words. Still, she isn't attacking me despite her instincts likely telling her to. I'm a predator, a threat to her. She should be attacking me. She should be fighting to get out of the cage.

"You are," I growl. "Accept her so we can move on."

Something snaps out of place and then snaps back, telling me Red attempted to force a change back and lost. Her wolf is too strong, fueled by her own strength and stubbornness. They're one. It's best to remain one.

"I. . .will. . .not," she spits, her throat thick with frustration.

Sighing, I reach into my pocket for the powder. I don't have much of it left. What I do have is simply left over from when Azalea gave me some too long ago to remember when. It was long before Dorothy came to Oz, long before even the Flamingo came to Oz. The Wizard had still been alive then, though as useless as he'd always been.

Without hesitation, I blow the dust into the wolf's face and watch as she drops to the ground, her change as painful each time as the first time. It will always be that way if she can't accept her wolf. The denial keeps the process from moving smoothly.

I stare down at Red on the ground panting in disappointment. Perhaps, she's not someone who can be helped. I have to keep the possibility in my head that it might be better to put her down rather than subject my people to her danger. I still have a duty to protect them first, no matter what I'd given up for them.

"Perhaps, a different approach," I say as she lays panting on the ground. She looks up at me with vibrant violet eyes, pretty if not for the fear there.

"What do you mean?" she pants.

"Follow me." I open the gate and walk out. I don't offer a hand to help her up. I don't wait to see if she follows. I know she will. As much as Red fears her wolf, she also fears what will become of her if I decide she's not worth the trouble. I'm already regretting my choice to barter with her but I'm curious enough about the meditation to give it a try.

I hear her following me a few seconds later, her feet dragging after the change. She likely already feels exhausted, but I'm not finished. The more she shifts, the more she tries to accept her wolf, the less exhausted she'll feel with each shift.

Without a word, I lead her out of the castle and into the street surrounding it. The market is taking place just as it always is, my people selling to each other each day. Sometimes, creatures from other quadrants come to purchase from the market but that doesn't happen as often anymore as it used to. We tend to stay within our own quadrants since Toto.

"What are we doing out here?" Red asks, confused. She's wearing the tattered remains of the shirt she'd been wearing but I don't offer a new one. She won't need it until after the next attempt. No use ruining two shirts.

I don't answer Red. Instead, I focus on the people in the street, my people. Once, before Toto, I used to consider some of them actual friends. Now, I'm so emotionless, I can't do much more than protect them as is my duty. A few familiar faces watch me carefully, flicking between where I stand and Red where she covers herself.

"Warning," I shout, loud enough that those in the street and stalls can hear me. They all pause what they're doing and watch me closely. "This woman is about to become her beast in an attempt to control herself. If you do not want to partake in her training, I suggest you lock yourselves in the nearest building immediately."

Red stiffens but I don't pay her any mind. Instead, I watch as a large group of people funnel into buildings and lock themselves away. Only a handful remain, including one man who used to be closer than a simple friend. Once upon a time, I'd shared ale with Lopper, the frog-like man standing in front of his stall, his webbed hands crossed primly over his front. I won't allow anything to happen to him or my other people, but Red doesn't need to know that.

"What is this?" Red hisses, her panic already filling her eyes.

I look over my shoulder at her. "Do you want to harm people?"

"Of course, not," she growls, looking at those who remain in the street.

"Then accept your wolf and don't harm my people."

Red's eyes widen at my words, and she looks over at the people again, the ones who are clearly not leaving despite the danger. "I'll kill them," she whispers, true fear in her eyes. There's the fear. She's not afraid of her wolf. She's afraid of the damage she does when the wolf is in charge.

"I'm sure their families will be very sad," I say coldly, making her eyes jerk back to mine. I know what she searches for. She's trying to find emotion in my eyes, but she won't find any. I know because I've spent too long searching my own mirror for the very same thing. It's not there. Not anymore.

Without waiting for her to panic and run away, I'm blowing more dust in her face, this time, the opposite. Instead of forcing her back to human, this dust forces her into a wolf, giving me control of her shift more than she has. She stumbles backward at the same time as her bones pop painfully, rapidly, speeding up the process. Instead of the normal minutes it takes her to transform, she stands wolven before me only a mere handful of seconds later, her body panting heavily in excruciating pain. Forcing such a fast change on someone who so clearly can't control herself will exhaust her. Likely, she'll sleep for another day after this, but it's necessary to drive home my point. Perhaps, she can control her wolf better, accept her, at the thought of killing an innocent person.

The moment she stands before me in her wolf form is the same moment her eyes change and Red no longer has control. I can feel her struggle, can sense it, but the change was too fast for her to get a grip on her wolf. Now, her wolf—Feral, as she calls her—is running the show.

She doesn't attack me, sensing me as a fellow predator. I don't run, don't cower. I simply watch her. The wolf, however, looks over me to my people and her eyes focus on Lopper, the closest person. Without a second's hesitation, she's running toward him, saliva dripping from her maw.

Lopper, to his credit, doesn't cower either. He simply stands there, watching this great hulking beast rushing toward him with intent to kill, calm as can be. He always was a strong character, always happy to help, so it shouldn't surprise me, but Red in her wolf form is scary for anyone not used to such predators.

I'm already moving the moment she goes for Lopper, already preparing to tackle her. She won't be able to gain control. I can feel her useless, weak struggle from here. There isn't enough time for her to gain control.

With a growl, I tackle the wolf to the ground, pinning her down just before she could have reached out her claws and dug them into Lopper. Even then, Lopper doesn't jump, not even when Red swipes out a claw and tries to sink them into his leg in order to drag him closer.

"Enough," I growl, blowing the last of the dust I possess in her face. Immediately, her bones begin to pop, and I get up, releasing her to change with painful aggression.

By the time she's human again, she's groaning and barely strong enough to lift herself on her elbows. She flops backward and looks up at Lopper, her face twisted with sorrow.

"I'm sorry," she rasps, apologizing to him, as if she can help her nature.

Lopper bows like the proper gentleman he is. "I had full faith in you, miss," he says, before meeting my eyes and bowing just the same out of respect. We haven't been as we were in too long, but still, I can't feel sadness as he walks away. I regret the loss, but I can't feel empathy toward the hurt he'd held in his own eyes.

When he's gone, Red looks up at me. The corners of her eyes are wet and I'm shocked that I didn't notice her crying until now, too lost in my own regret to care about hers.

"I'm a monster," she whispers, beginning to shiver.

Without a word, I pull my shirt off and pass it to her, waiting for her to pull it on before I reply. Once she's covered and drags herself to shaking legs, I meet her eyes without flinching.

"You will always be a monster, Red," I say, and she visibly jerks back form my words. "There is no turning back from it anymore." I glance after Lopper again, but he's already gone, off to do whatever it is he's filled his life with. "But what type of monster you become is entirely up to you."

Red blinks at me, at the words I speak, as if it hadn't dawned on her that she can choose her monster. We all have the capability to be either good or evil at any point in time. Not all monsters are evil. Not all humans are good.

I don't add anything else. Instead, I turn to walk away, leaving her standing there on the yellow brick road. I should probably tell her not to stand there for too long or else the yellow brick road begins to hunger but she can figure it out herself.

Warring with the decision to allow her to live, to keep helping her, I enter my castle and disappear inside, needing a break from it all.

"*Helping her is a good thing*," the voice murmurs. "*Imagine how you'd feel about it if you could feel.*"

"That's the problem," I growl. "I feel nothing one way or the other." Sighing, I run a hand through my hair. "It doesn't matter."

But I can't quite understand why I want to help her to begin with if I don't care how she feels. Something niggles in my mind but it's fleeting, and I've forgotten it a few seconds later.

In the end, I convince myself it's my duty as an Heir to neutralize a threat and that's the only reason I'm helping.

Yes, that's the only reason I'm helping.

CHAPTER FOURTEEN

ANANKE

The throne I sit in is crumbling and decrepit but it's still mine. The castle still sits in the unruled quadrant of Oz, the Heirs not thinking to look for me in the place they think I escaped. Though my castle is no longer the glorious structure it once was, it's still my home. Thorny vines climb through the entire area, pushing stone aside to take over. They're the only thing that give me chills about my home, not because of the thorns, but because I remember what it feels like to have them crawling along my skin as I slept.

Just because I'd been sleeping, doesn't mean I wasn't aware of everything going on around me. I felt it all, felt the vines crawling along my body and cocooning me within them. I'd ripped them to shreds when I'd woken but nothing can be done for the concavities in my flesh where they'd permanently marked me. It all remains hidden for now save for a small mark on my cheek. I can't have anyone seeing my punishment written in my skin. I don't want to show that weakness.

In the other room, I can hear Hansel and Gretel bickering between them, arguing over something foolish. This time, I think it's something to do with an accidental step, but I can't be sure. The siblings fight for every reason. If I didn't need them for my plan, I'd have already killed them for simply being annoying.

My nails tap against the weathered stone of my throne, leaving behind tiny marks in the rock where my claws hit. Once upon a time, I'd had soft nails, nails fit for a princess, but those days are long gone. Now, they're hard enough to slice like knives. I don't understand why anyone warned away from such power. I'd gained the ability to seek out my vengeance. If only the one person I want to kill was still alive.

Rumple comes in through the door, his steps slow and unhurried. The trickster stops far away, hesitant to get too close to me and the power that crackles through the air. He's smart, smarter than the siblings, but still, he's not like us. Where we're World Breakers, Rumpelstiltskin is simply a nuisance and nothing more. Every day, he speaks less and less, only using his voice when necessary. If he weren't such a good messenger and spy, I'd have already killed him. Still, once we went to war, he'll be useless to me. He doesn't need to know that, however. The best way to keep a man from wanting to escape a cage is for him to think there's no cage at all.

"You bring news?" I ask when he doesn't immediately speak, waiting for me to speak first. Clever of him. He doesn't do it out of respect. He does so out of self-preservation.

"There's talk of a woman appearing in Winkie Country and the Lion has taken her into his home for some reason."

The corner of my lip curls up. "You have proof?"

He hesitates for a few seconds. "Only hearsay from a few different resources. I know nothing about the woman herself, but I'd place merit on the rumors." He keeps his hands folded behind him, a picture of calm as he says, "The Lion is aware of our plan. I'd be willing to bet he's taken precautions—"

I wave away his words of advice. Normally, I wouldn't explain myself, but it's good for my messenger to know what to look for when searching for rumors. "It matters not if he's taken precautions," I murmur. "Prophesy is prophesy, and no man can turn away someone meant to share his heart, not matter what he's given up."

Rumple tilts his head, curious. For a moment, I think he won't be brave enough to ask, but he surprises me when he does. "You speak as if you know firsthand."

Those words are all it takes for my eyes to glaze over and a picture to appear in my mind. Dark chocolate eyes appear there, both a temptation and a mockery. "I do," I find myself saying. "His name was Phillip." But then my eyes clear and the memory dissipates. "Go. Find more information and see if things can be hurried along. I doubt we will have to do anything, but this is a game of chess." I gesture toward the other room where Hansel and Gretel still argue. "Take those two with you and send them in to cause trouble. Trouble always brews closeness."

Rumple scowls at me, forgetting for a moment who I am. "I don't want to take those two id—"

Power crackles from me, snapping out at him and causing him to jump backward to avoid certain death. He clamps his mouth shut and bows his head.

I nod and lean back in my throne with a smile, closing my eyes to the image of the trickster going to the other room to gather the siblings. I don't sleep, not anymore. I slept too long before. Now, I need action, not rest. But still, the memories have been awakened in my mind, and I can't help seeing the eyes again, the face, but some of the features are fuzzy. It's been so long I can barely remember. . .

Soon, the Lion will fall, and Toto will be free to join us, to destroy Oz and burn down the rest of the worlds with me. They will all pay for what they'd done, for what they continue to do. I'll make sure of it.

I hear the others leave and then I'm alone in the large castle with only the thorny vines to keep my company. Down the long hallway, in the distance, I hear the soft cry of a baby just barely born, a phantom that echoes through the walls, but I don't go to investigate. I don't move at all.

No phantom will sway me today.

Still, my heart gives a painful throb in my chest, and I find myself pressing my hand against my achingly flat stomach. Because no one is there to witness it, I allow a single tear to fall.

CHAPTER FIFTEEN

RED

I'd slept for too many hours after the "help" King deigned to give me, the exhaustion making it impossible to do anything more than pass out. It seems I'll be sleeping it off each time I struggle with my change. Whatever King is attempting to teach me, I'm not sure if there will ever be a time where I can shift into Feral and not be so tired that it leaves me at a disadvantage. Will I grow stronger with each change so that eventually, shifting won't leave me weak? I hope so.

Currently, King is staring at me from across the table, his large claw tapping at the wood in a constant rhythm that's starting to grate on my nerves. We haven't spoken since we sat down and food was placed before us. I've mostly ignored the arrogant bastard, choosing to primly pick at the meat on the table. Since I'm no longer starving, I'm attempting to not eat like a wild animal, but the temptation to rip it to shreds is still so strong, I have to focus in order to keep my bites slow and meticulous. I can still eat like a proper human but it's so difficult, I end up tuning everything out around me without meaning to. For that reason, when King finally speaks, I nearly jump in my seat.

"How did you become your beast?" he asks, his voice echoing in the quiet chamber.

I freeze at his question, at the flashes of memory it attempts to manifest. For the briefest moment, I get a flash of golden eyes, but I shove it down so brutally, I'm able to pretend it never happened at all.

"That's personal," I say long seconds later, not daring to look up at him. Instead, I stare steadily at my plate.

He hums. "Then, I'm to assume it was traumatic." When I glance up at his words, he nods. "That makes sense."

"You don't know anything about me," I growl. I don't particularly like someone attempting to figure me out, searching for answers to questions he has no business finding. Hell, I haven't even found some of those answers. And King is an asshole. I'd rather he not know precisely what I'm thinking at all times.

King shrugs and tears a piece of meat from the bone before popping it in his mouth. When he finishes chewing, the corner of his lips curl just barely at me, as if I amuse him. "I know everything I need to."

"Fuck you," I spit, baring my teeth in a threat.

King's face changes, and somehow, he looks like a different, harsher person. I'm almost not surprised when his voice comes out thicker. I barely question his strangeness anymore. "Well, I certainly wouldn't be opposed."

I blink at the man sitting before me. "I'm sorry. What?"

The grin on his face turns saccharine, a tease, and I'm surprised by the switch from cold and unfeeling to predatory and promiscuous. "Perhaps, I can tame your beast, little wolf."

"With your *dick*?" I scowl at him, my food forgotten on my plate at his words. "You're awfully confident in your skills there, buddy."

He shrugs. "The offer is there if you'd ever like to take it." He clears his throat and the next time he speaks, his voice is normal, and the seductive expression is gone. "I helped you yesterday. Today you help me. You promised to teach me meditation."

Narrowing my eyes on him, I push my plate forward and cross my arms. "Are you going to make more inappropriate comments?"

"Most likely." Though his words say one thing, his tone says another. He's back to the emotionless King, and I'm not sure how I feel about the wishy-washy personality. Am I to believe the cold mask or the seductive asshole?

"At least you'll have to be quiet for meditation," I growl, standing up. I leave my food unfinished on my plate, eager to hold up my end of the deal and no longer feel as if I'm using him. "Let's do it then."

Thirty minutes later, I'm regretting every decision I've ever made that's led me to this moment. I'm not only frustrated, but I'm highly annoyed by the man sitting cross-legged beside me. By sheer willpower alone, I haven't gutted him with my claws and stormed off into the forest. I'd almost prefer the danger of the jungle to sitting through more torture such as this.

My eyes are closed as I attempt to sink inside the place in me that allows calmness. It had taken me longer to learn how to reach that place after I'd shifted for the first time, but once I found it, it was like remembering a feeling after that. As long as everything is silent, I can find my way there.

"This is foolish," King growls from beside me. He should have his eyes closed while he takes deep breaths but instead, when I open my eyes with a scowl, he's staring right back at me with those golden eyes.

"If you'd ever shut up for longer than a minute, we might be able to actually meditate." My words are full of my frustration and ire, but King either doesn't notice or he doesn't care. I'm willing to bet on the later.

"I knew this would be pointless," he grunts, and I almost hear disappointment there. "Just a trick of the weak apparently."

I attempt to clear my mind before I respond so I don't insult him. He's my host, after all. I breathe through my nose, a long, drawn-out breath, and release it in a quick burst.

"I thought you said to exhale for five seconds," he comments.

Throwing my hands in the air, I give up the pretense of trying to find my calm place. I'll never be able to with him beside me. "For ever-loving fuck's sake, shut the fuck up!" I spit, unfolding my legs. "You insufferable, ignorant, wet towel!"

King stiffens. "What did you just call me?"

I almost laugh. It's clear he doesn't understand the insult and so he's not only challenging me, but genuinely asking me what I'd called him. Pity for him, I don't care to explain.

Meeting his eyes, I bare my teeth. "Teach yourself to meditate. I'm done."

"You're done when I say you're done," he growls.

Leaping to my feet, I move to put distance between us before I do something foolish. I can feel Feral taking notice inside me, can feel her urge to attack and react to my emotions. Mentally, I pet her, trying to calm her down, but she's restless and understandably so.

"I'm talking to you!" King speaks from behind me, obviously following.

"Fuck off!" I snarl.

Sharp claws wrap around my wrist, halting my escape as he jerks me around to face him. When our eyes meet, I know mine are golden with my wolf just beneath the surface. I want to rip him to shreds, to give him a taste of his own medicine, but I attempt to calm Feral, instead. I can't have her always springing forward any time I'm high on emotions. I'm far too short-tempered a person to give her that control.

"I said stay." A command, but I'm no coward. I'm not backing down from this asshole. He doesn't own me despite offering me a safe place. None of that entitles him to my body.

"And I said go fuck yourself!"

I kick him, hard, right in the center of his chest. My mother would have been proud of the kick—she'd spent hours teaching me the proper way once—and an image of her face passes across my mind. More anger fills me.

King doesn't release me with the impact. Instead, his hand tightens around my wrist, keeping me still, his face pinched in anger. It's a nice change from the emotionless mask he wears like a shield normally.

Fur climbs my arms, the change pushing forward. I coo to Feral in my mind, but the fur stays. However, I don't exactly start shifting. I want to hurt King, to teach him a lesson though, so for the first time ever, I call my wolf forward. I invite Feral to the forefront and my arm changes. My fingers tip with claws. Muscle thickens my appendage as the bones pop and lengthen. The moment it's finished changing, I swipe at him. His only defense is to release me and jump backwards or risk a cut down his face to match the one already there.

The grin that splits his mouth infuriates me.

I push Feral forward more and my other arms lengthens. My teeth sharpen in my mouth, cutting into my too human lips. King, as usual, doesn't change at all, and I wonder against what sort of beast he is. He's no wolf. Not only does he not smell like one, but he admitted he wasn't the same as me. The question is, what sort of beast does he hide within himself? A lion like those carved into his crown? But then why never change?

When I lunge at the bastard, he has the audacity to chuckle as he dances out of the way, as if we're playing a game and I'm not trying to gut him. I won't kill him, but I want to hurt him enough that he rethinks calling me weak. When I grab for him, he instead wraps his own claws around both of my wrists, holding me prone.

"Let me go," I snarl, fighting to get him off me so I can continue trying to rip him to shreds. I'm angry and frustrated, and it only makes me feel desperate to prove myself more.

"Look at you," he purrs. "You're finally accepting your wolf."

The moment King points it out is the moment I realize what I'm doing. I'm half transformed at my behest, Feral holding herself back but allowing me to use her weapons. Revulsion hits me at the sudden monstrousness of it. The moment I realize is the moment I lose control and I can no longer hold the half-shift. I'm both terrified of what I am and intrigued, but I can't accept what that makes me, not yet. I shove hard against Feral, making her whimper in my mind and withdraw, but not before she takes some of my strength with her for the slight.

I meet King's eyes with a hard gaze, despite my sudden exhaustion. "I'm human," I announce, as if that's the answer to all my questions. It's my final cling to my humanity, as silly as that is.

Releasing my wrists, he steps back. "Sooner or later, your human side loses. It always does." His words are heavy but soft, a different voice that I've never heard before. It's all in the tone, and it suddenly feels like I'm speaking to a different person yet again, but different to the other two. "But we all have the possibility for both human and monster. It lives in all of us. Your responsibility is deciding the balance between them."

His words hit me hard. They pierce through my ribs and sit heavy in my chest, hanging there for me to mull over later when I'm alone and plagued by nightmares. I take a step back, putting more distance between us.

"We'll continue meditation tomorrow," King says, turning to walk away.

I scowl at his back. "Like hell we will."

"When the sun hits the water fountain, meet me," he continues as if I didn't speak.

"Did you not hear me?" I growl, crossing my arms.

He looks over his shoulder at me, his face cold. "Oh, I heard you, little wolf," he says. "I just don't care."

He leaves me outside the castle scowling at his back and I've never wanted to hit someone over the head more than I do the King of Winkie Country.

"Fucking asshole," I growl, before making my own way inside the castle with a huff.

CHAPTER SIXTEEN

Perry is lying in the bed beside me, his breathing deep and even, telling me he's asleep while I'm lying in bed staring at the ceiling. I rub my thighs together in agitation, glancing up at him in the dim light of the room. With a soft shush of sound, I twist in the sheets and reach over toward him, running my fingers along his hip bone softly until he stirs. When he shifts in the sheets and one of his eyes crack open just barely, I reach lower, circling his length and stroking.

"Well, good morning to you, too," he whispers, his voice husky with both sleep and desire as his length comes to life in my hand.

My lips curl as I shift again, moving to climb on top of him. Though it's typically frowned upon to have sex before we're married, Perry and I had never followed those rules. I don't worry he will leave me. I don't worry about my reputation, much to my mother's dismay. What point is there to remain "pure" and "chaste" if I don't really care to be either of those things? Instead of worrying about it, we both fall into each other every night and hold the other close enough to share air.

Perry's rough fingers stroke along my thighs before settling on my hips as I lift myself above him and line his length up with my throbbing entrance.

"Do you love me?" I ask, hovering there, teasing.

"Like you're the only star in the sky," he replies, the sweet smile on his face one I've come to know. Though he throbs in my hand, Perry doesn't push, doesn't rush. The way he looks up at me, as if I'm beautiful, makes something inside me purr. Despite his sweetness, I still can't call the feeling inside me love. I want it to be love, but it isn't. I don't know what it is. Maybe it's some need to win the competition for his heart. Maybe I'm just a bad person who wants him to want me so much, it hurts.

Perry doesn't ask me the same question in return. I think, deep down, he knows the struggle I have and hopes one day I'll simply fall in love with him. I'm fond of him. I adore him. But do I love him? I don't think this is what love should feel like.

Carefully, I lower myself on his length, letting him slide home in my wetness, and we both moan in pleasure at the feeling. His fingers tighten on my hips, almost too hard, and when there's a prick of pain there, I look down in the midst of grinding against him in curiosity. Instead of the rough human fingers I know, there are claws there, nicking my skin, drawing a few tiny beads of blood.

"Perry. . ."

When I meet his eyes again, they're ringed with gold. I pause but the claws at my hip urge me to keep going, grinding me down hard against him.

"Tell me you love me," he growls, his voice beastly.

"Stop," I command, trying to get off him, jerking away, but his claws hold me where he wants me. He continues to pump inside me despite my struggle. Perry has always been strong, but not this strong.

"Tell me you love me, Scarlett," he snarls. "Tell me you'll never leave me."

I watch in horror as his features start to change, as he becomes more beast than man, and I struggle harder, desperate to get away, desperate to ignore the popping bones.

"I'll make sure you stay with me forever," he groans, and then those teeth snap out and sink into my shoulder, the crunch of bone and skin making me scream out in terror and pain. I'm screaming, fighting, the pain almost unbearable as he sinks in deeper. "Mine," he says around the bite. "You're mine."

69

The room changes, brightens, and I blink at the sudden absence of pain. I press my hand to my shoulder only to find smooth, unblemished skin. When I look down at Perry in confusion again, he's not there. Instead, brilliant golden eyes meet mine, a scar bisecting one and making it cloudy.

"Hello, little wolf," King purrs.

I'm straddling him, his length nestled between my thighs, and without a second thought, I start moving on him, rocking my hips. This time, when claws dig into my hips, I pay them no mind, the pinch of pain welcome. Moaning, I grind against him, relishing the soft thrusts of his own hips. Digging my own claws along his skin, I move faster, the sounds of our joining filling the room and only adding to the dirtiness of it.

"Yes," he groans. "Claim me, little wolf. Make me yours. . ."

I JERK AWAKE SO HARD, I THROW PILLOWS OFF THE BED, MY BREATH coming out erratically as the images of the dream fill my mind. My body is still flushed, the erotic memories hitting me just right. When I rub my thighs together, I realize it wasn't all necessarily a dream. My body is still reacting to the thoughts as if I want exactly what I'd seen. Since when had my nightmares turned into. . .that?

Movement from the doorway has me freezing before jerking up the sheets to cover more of my flushed skin, hiding my naked breasts from the man standing there.

"What are you going here?" I hiss, pressing my thighs together tighter in the hopes it will hide my scent. Predators always had heightened sense of smell and King is certainly one of those even if I don't know exactly what kind yet. I'm starting to suspect the lions on his crown aren't just for decoration, thinking he's called the Lion by the people in the street for a reason, but I've never seen a lion, only a man.

"You were screaming," he answers, studying me. "I thought there was a threat, but when I got here, I saw the threat was only in your mind." His head tilts to the side. "I was turning to go, but. . ."

I frown. "But what?"

The shadows dance along his face as he shifts in the darkness, the only light streaming in through the window making him look more frightening. Too bad I'm not scared of this monster. The only monster I fear lives inside my head.

"Your screams and cries of pain. . .turned to moans of pleasure." He raises his brow at me. "Anything I should know about?"

"No," I growl, but I can't hide the flush that dances along my cheeks at the thought of him hearing me moaning. The imagery of me riding the man before me flashes through my mind again, making the flush deepen. Damn it all. This isn't something I want the asshole knowing.

A slow, smug smile curls his lips, as if he knows exactly what's causing it, but he doesn't address my clear discomfort. Instead, he says, "don't forget to meet for meditation."

"I'd rather vomit," I respond on instinct, because how can I sit beside this man with the images in my mind now?

"I don't care," I replies, but his tone is less cold. When he leaves, he closes the door behind him.

Only then do I slump back down in the bed and cover my face.

"You're an idiot," I tell myself. "True and honestly an idiot."

But the image of King beneath me pops into my mind again, his words, and I can't stop myself from reaching beneath the sheets and finishing the job myself.

CHAPTER SEVENTEEN

S itting out in the grass with King is a unique experience when I'm trying my hardest not to think about him telling me to claim him. Trying to mask my scent so he doesn't smell my arousal is a whole different challenge when sitting cross-legged beside him. In the end, I find myself putting distance between us in the hopes it'll help. I doubt it does. Unless King is a useless predator, he's going to be able to smell it. I just hope he doesn't realize it's because of him. Some petty part of me wants to bring him down a notch.

"Breathe in for five," I murmur, my eyes closed against the dim light of Oz. I miss the sun. though the Grimm forest is. . .well, grim, every now and then, the sun comes out and shines through the trees. I've yet to see the sun here in Oz, as if it doesn't exist here. Oz is meant to be dark. "Breathe out for five."

I hear King follow my directions, for once being quiet enough that I think we might actually make some progress. For whatever reason, he's decided to be less an asshole today. I'm not going to question it in case the universe decides to mock me and stir him up again.

"Imagine yourself sinking into a cloud, or a large, soft pillow. Keep breathing until you feel yourself relax so deeply, you could almost fall asleep."

I keep my voice soft and gentle, the only thing that relaxes Feral completely. Inside me, I feel her consciousness curl up and fall asleep. Her normal restlessness disappears and I'm able to breathe without her stomping around. The tension in my shoulders and neck eases until I almost feel normal.

Almost.

Carefully, I open my eyes and look over at King to make sure he's doing okay. His eyes are closed, his body relaxed. He's almost more beautiful like this. Rather than looking cold and emotionless, he appears serene. His shoulder-length hair gently moves with the slight wind sweeping around us. The crown he always wears sits in the grass beside him, less weight on his head to help with relaxation. The rings on his fingers still somehow glitter despite the lack of sunshine. Even like this, he looks regal, just as a King is meant to appear.

"I can feel you looking at me," he mumbles.

"Just making sure you're doing it right."

"It's not difficult," he replies. And then, his voice changes into a softer one, a different weight in tone. "I like this."

My brows furrow. "Meditation?"

"Us, spending time together."

My brows shoot up in surprise. "Oh?"

Then, harsher, he says, "It would be better naked." The other voice I've heard.

Recognizing that I'm suddenly giving these different tones a completely different personality each, I scowl. "What's happening right now?"

"Nothing," King's voice answers, and his eyes pop open, but his head twitches to the side and his face softens again. "He doesn't know what he's talking about. Too scared to admit we enjoy spending time with you."

"I. . ." I stare at the man before me, blinking. "I'm confused."

"Of course you are," he growls, thick voice again. "I'm Fang. Nice to meet you."

My mouth pops open. "But I thought you were King."

"I am King," he growls, but the voice doesn't stay, as if he can't necessarily control it. "Meditating makes it possible for us to come forward easier," the softer voice takes over. "I'm Ophir by the way."

73

"Ophir. . ."

He moves then, his face twisting until I know it's Fang looking at me. Uncrossing his legs, he's suddenly leaping across the distance. I'm too shocked to react in a way I should have, so when he pushes me backward, I'm on my back in the grass before I realize what's happened. He hovers over me, his fierce eyes tracing over my body. For a moment, I don't even fight, still too surprised to fully comprehend what's exactly is happening.

"A pretty thing like you would look beautiful on her knees," Fang murmurs, his eyes taking in everything about me.

It's strange to recognize I'm talking to someone else despite him having the same face as King. I've never encountered something like this, but his words penetrate through my surprise, breaking my shock. My face pinches into a scowl.

Without waiting for more words, I'm flipping us, until I'm on top of him, looking down at the Lion with my teeth bared. "I scratch and bite," I warn.

His hands grab at my waist, reminding me of the dream. I can't stop the flush on my cheeks, and it only gets worse when he responds. His eyes greedily drink me in.

"You'll beg and crawl, too," he promises with a purr.

My core clenches at his words. Those words shouldn't be sexy. I shouldn't be straddling his waist and feeling his length against my core through our clothing. I shouldn't be *liking* it.

Fang flickers away and his face softens. Ophir. "Sorry about Fang," Ophir apologizes. "He's a neanderthal."

I blink down at him, at the sweeter one who still doesn't release my hips. In fact, his hands gently slide along my thighs, leaving trails of fire in their wake. "I. . ." I don't even know what to say.

His expression drops all emotion and I realize King is back, golden eyes looking up at me. "Stop," he growls, but I don't necessarily think he's speaking to me. His hands fall away from my thighs before he shoves me off his lap. I'm still so shocked at everything, I fall ungracefully to the side with an oomph.

I stare at him with wide eyes. "There's three of you," I breathe.

King scowls and stands, his movement far more fluid than my own.

My eyes dance to the crown still sitting on the ground where three very distinct lion heads are displayed. It's practically there in plain sight, for all to see.

Leaping to my feet, I stare at him and repeat my words. "There's three of you."

"So what?" he growls, and there's a hint of something in his voice. Not panic exactly, but perhaps, hesitation.

Tilting my head to the side to better study him, I frown. "Is it a secret?"

For a moment, he doesn't say anything. Then his eyes meet mine, and he admits softly, "yes".

I purse my lips. Here's something I can hold over him, can use to my advantage, but I'm not that person. I'm not a blackmailer. My mother would have told me to use whatever tools I can to protect myself, but King hasn't hurt me. He's been an absolute asshole, sure, but otherwise, he poses no danger to me.

"Your secret is safe with me," I finally reply.

He looks at me sharply. "Why?"

Sighing, I run a hand through my long hair and look down. "Because I understand wanting to keep something close." When he still stares at me and I see his tension from beneath my lashes, I sigh again. "Perhaps, I should tell you my story, after all. To make it fair."

CHAPTER EIGHTEEN

WENDY DARLING

I'm sitting outside the Tin Man's home, my eyes on Aniya where she sits with her animals. She's talking to them, these creatures fully capable of hurting her if they want to. I've always been curious about the child of Tiger Lily and Peter Pan, what kind of creature she will be once she fully matures, but the more time I spend with her, the less worried I get. She has all the same humanity we all do.

Aniya still grows at an accelerated rate but not nearly as fast as she had been in Neverland. Jupiter thinks she'll slow once she reaches a certain age and simply stop aging. No one really knows but, as it is, Aniya now appears around fourteen, a young woman. She's beautiful —not that I expect anything less from the child of Tiger and Peter— and powerful beyond compare.

As I watch her, Aniya looks up at me and smiles softly. The ground just barely rumbles in answer. A World Breaker, we all suspect. How can someone like her not be that powerful? But she is and continues to be raised with love. Perhaps, a World Breaker is shaped by their upbringing more than anything else. After all, everyone has the potential to be evil just as much as the potential to be good. It makes sense that it will be the same for Aniya.

The front door of Tin's home opens and Clara waddles out, her stomach so large now, it's clear she's due any day. I don't particularly know the time frame of pregnancy in a world such as this, but it's best to be on guard for any moment.

Clara, when she sees me sitting out on the bench, waddles over and takes a seat.

"You shouldn't be outside," I tell her, smiling gently to let her know I mean no offense. "The Hatter will—"

"I'm not fragile," Clara grumbles, rubbing her belly. "I need some air is all. This baby is pushing on my ribs, and it hurts like a bitch."

In her pregnancy, Clara has gotten less proper with her speech the further along she grows. No one blames her. Creating life is a blessing and a curse. At least, that's what I think after watching my mother give birth to my two younger brothers so long ago. That's the extent of my knowledge. At least, Tiger has been through it so she can help Clara during the process. Jupiter will help, too, though she isn't a doctor. Her scientific experience makes her more equipped than anyone of us. I certainly know nothing about birthing babies.

Hatter is driving everyone mad with his frantic nesting and preparations. He'd carved a crib from an entire fallen tree just the other day and then tore through one of Tin's walls to get it inside when it proved too big for the door. Tin had lost his mind and only after Briella Mae calmed him down did things get better. He'll make a good father, but if he has his choice, Clara would currently be inside a bubble resting while he waits on her hand and foot. Their love is something to be envied, and I would envy them if I didn't have the same type of relationship with Hook. Even now, my eyes trace over to where my Captain of the Stars helps with war preparations. For a second, I'm impossibly glad that I'm not in the same situation as Clara right now.

"You won't be able to fight like that," I comment, glancing down at Clara's belly. Even if she were able to, Hatter will never allow her to go into battle as vulnerable as she is.

"I know," Clara sighs. "If this baby could just last until after the war that's coming to make his or her appearance, that would be great, but that sort of luck rarely follows me."

Her words feel like prophesy, and I tuck them away for later.

Likely, something like that will come to pass. We can only hope that things don't descend into chaos at the worst time.

Clara shifts on her seat, as if she can't quite get comfortable. When she looks at me, I see a question hanging there. Just when I think she won't ask, she says, "Have you noticed feeling. . .strange?"

I tilt my head. "Strange how?"

"More powerful?"

It takes everything in me to school my features. "No, why?"

Clara waves her hand as if to dismiss it. "No reason," she murmurs. "I better get back inside before Hatter discovers I'm gone and starts a man hunt." Her giggle makes something inside me warm. Though she's annoyed by his doting, there's clear adoration in those words. "I love the man, but he's being entirely too overprotective with this baby."

"Can you blame him?" I ask with a smile.

"No," Clara sighs. "Be careful out here."

And then she stands and waddles back inside, a harbinger of new life that we all need to protect. Clara will serve as the second to bring in a new era, and with that will come new events none of us are prepared for. Still, none of us shy away from that responsibility. I press my hand against my flat stomach. I don't know if one day I'll follow in her footsteps, but for now, I'm happy to simply help her with her journey.

Once I'm sure Clara is gone, I glance down at the tiny droplets of water dancing along the ground around me. Frowning, I shoo them with my hand. "Go away," I grunt.

Without hesitation, the water disappears back into the ground, but it doesn't make me feel any better.

After all, I've never been able to control water so easily before. . .

CHAPTER NINETEEN

RED

I stare at King across the long table, amused that we always seem to find ourselves at this very same table, eating. I suppose, for predators, it's important to eat. How many meals a day do we eat? I'm not even sure. My measurement of time has been skewed after my long stint as Feral.

King twitches where he's sitting, his head tilting to the side as if he's listening to someone speak. It's only as he does it that I realize he's probably talking to Fang and Ophir. I still can't quite wrap my mind around the thought that there are three distinct people inside King. Is it a very real situation or is he crazy? There had once been a lady in my village who suffered a similar ailment, but it had been determined by the town doctor she was simply mad. Could he have been wrong? Could she have been telling the truth?

"I'm not a freak show," King snarls suddenly, his teeth bared at me.

I frown. "I never said you were."

"Then stop looking at me like that." He crosses his arms over his chest, as if for protection, but he has no need to protect himself from me. It takes a lot for me to admit it to myself, but King is stronger than me. I'll never admit that out loud, though. It would only make his already inflated ego larger.

"I'm curious, is all," I murmur, lying my elbows on the table despite knowing how rude it is. King, to his credit, doesn't seem to care. He never seems to care about anything at all.

"You said you were going to tell me your story," he replies, his face hard. He doesn't gesture for me to speak, doesn't rush me, but he's clearly waiting.

With a sigh, I pick up a small piece of meat and nod.

"You're right. I told you I understand wanting to keep secrets, and this is one I'd prefer to keep inside, but it's only fair I share something now that you have, though I'd like to point out you didn't willingly tell me your secret and I'm doing so."

King rolls his eyes. "Yes, of course. That makes you a better person than me. Now continue." His words are sarcastic, but I don't let them bother me. At this point, it's simply a part of his personality.

"I wasn't always a wolf. In fact, I was once achingly human. In the Grimm Forest, werewolves are a common sight, and I was trained from a young age to hunt them when necessary."

"Who trained you?" he asks, leaning forward in his chair.

"My mother. When she was younger, she was famed for her hunting skills. It was her who used to have me wear a red cloak. For protection, she'd say. I never put much merit in it, and after I became. . .this, I placed even less in it." Sighing, I sat back in my chair and pull my hair over my shoulder where I start braiding it as a distraction from the memories. "Perry Holland was the blacksmith in our village. We grew up together, were the same age, and it was widely agreed upon in the village that he was the most eligible bachelor. He had a respectable job, made good money, but passed that, he was a genuinely good person. He was kind and sweet. . .and that was probably why no one ever suspected him. I certainly didn't and we dated for years with the full intention to marry. He was in love with me, despite what the other villagers thought of me, and no matter how much I knew I didn't return the feelings, I was fond of him. He was a good steady choice."

"An easy choice," King nodded. "I understand that."

"Easy, yes," I agree. "My mother was delighted with the choice, and it was just a matter of waiting for Perry to propose. It went well until he asked me to run away with him on the night of a full moon. I declined, not because I didn't care, but because I cared for my mother more. I explained I couldn't leave her. She was older, was no longer working the same. I supported her with my hunting, and I explained there was no reason to leave. I thought he accepted my answer, but he hadn't, not really." I paused, biting my lip at the memories. Closing my eyes against them because I owe King the story, I continue. "We were being. . .intimate, when Perry changed. It was small at first. His eyes glowed and then sharp claws appeared. I tried to leave, realizing him for what he was, but it was still Perry. I thought perhaps he would be safer because he loved me. Instead, in his twisted mind, biting me was the only way to keep me." Gently, I pulled aside my shirt to show the scar on my shoulder, large bite marks. "While I was writhing in pain and panicking, he left me. I attempted to hurt him. I hunted so many werewolves before so it should have been easy."

"But you cared for him," King murmurs.

Nodding, I move my shirt back into place. "I hesitated when I had my chance, and in response, he went and killed my mother, so I no longer have a reason to stay. We fought, and in my grief, I shoved a silver dagger through his heart and pushed him off a cliff."

King watches me carefully, his eyes tracing over my face. "And so you became the very thing you hunted."

"The first time I changed, I was still hiding in my mother's house, trying to find the strength to end myself for everyone's benefit, but I waited too long. The full moon forced my change, and in the middle of the night, I slaughtered my entire village. I woke up in a pool of blood, soaked in it, the bodies of those I killed strewn around me like some sort of macabre artwork. Feral's belly was sated so I was very much human when I ran and ran and ran until I couldn't anymore." My eyes meet his. "I'm no stranger to what I am."

For a moment, he simply stares at me. It shouldn't surprise me when he's still the asshole but somehow, it does. "So, I was right about the trauma."

I roll my eyes, annoyed. "Maybe. But we all have trauma." I reach for more meat and pop it in my mouth, trying my hardest not to remember the images of my dead and burning village, of shoving a blade through my boyfriend's chest, of finding my mother's body shredded beyond repair as she breathed her last breath.

"We all rise from our worst disasters," King says suddenly, drawing my attention. "We turn. We change. We become. There's nothing wrong with that."

Something passes between us, a shared moment, that I don't fully understand. My chest grows warm with his attention, with the idea that, perhaps, being what I am isn't so bad. Inevitability is a part of life. Sometimes, things are meant to happen exactly as they do.

It's only as I'm staring at him, wondering exactly what life has planned for me, that I realize how vulnerable I'm being. Because I'm focused on him, it takes me longer to sense that something is wrong. King hears it first, the sounds of someone shouting. I hear it a second later, my head tilting in confusion as someone laughs maliciously outside the window to our left.

"What is that?" I go to ask, but I don't get the words out before something is thrown in the window. I leap to my feet, my eyes on the small bundle smoking on the floor. I have barely a half-second to wonder at what it can be before it reveals itself. With a loud crack, the bundle explodes in a brilliant light of magic and heat. I fly backward, slamming into the opposite wall at my back and sliding down. My ears ring with a shrill tone, my head full of fuzz. Dust rains down in the room around us, evidence of the explosion. I stand and stumble over the chair I'd vacated before, and everything changes around me at the suddenness of the attack. I'm no longer seeing King's castle. I'm standing in my village, the people I'd grown up with, had liked, strewn around me in pieces. Things are burning. Eyes are staring at me in horror. I'm a monster, a monster, a monster.

Gasping, I jerk backward, attempting to get away from the memories. I see two people outside the window, a male and a female, cackling as they dart into the trees, but they don't register as a threat. I'm the threat. I'm the monster here.

"Little wolf," someone says, but when I look at King, I don't see him. Instead, I see Perry, grinning at me with a dagger shoved through his chest. "You're mine, Scarlett," he says, and I rear back in horror.

"I killed you," I croak, stumbling away, desperate to get away from the phantom.

Trauma, fear, pain, it all slams inside me. I don't belong to him. I can't. I won't.

With a howl of sorrow as my bones begin to snap, I burst through the door of the castle and take off into the poisonous jungle, desperate to run from myself.

CHAPTER TWENTY

KING

I curse Hansel and Gretel as they take off into the jungle, tempted to go after them but knowing I have a more pressing matter to attend to. I'd seen Red's face, had seen the past flickering in her eyes. She's out there, forced into her werewolf form, locked in a living nightmare she'd tried her hardest to get rid of. Though I don't care about her in particular—I try to convince myself—I can't have a beast running rampant like that. She'll kill anything that walks in her path and we're already preparing for war. We need fighters, and if she kills them, we'll have less chances of winning. We need her on our side. That's what I tell myself.

With a snarl, I chase after the wolf, determined to bring her back and lock her up until she gains her senses. Her trauma is ruling her mind, and though I don't know much about helping trauma, I have to try.

"*She's hurting,*" Ophir murmurs. "*We should help her.*"

"How?" I growl. "Now would be the time for bright ideas."

"*Just be there for her,*" he counters in annoyance. "*It's not difficult.*"

"You forget he has no empathy," Fang interrupts. *"It could go either way. He could just as easily make things worse."*

I follow her scent, chasing after her through a jungle that shrinks away from my presence. They don't dare attack me, knowing it will spell their doom, so they make room for me as I pass, practically leading me to her without me having to use my senses at all. Still, her smell permeates the air, urging me forward.

Red's fast, faster than I expect, so it surprises me that I even catch up to her when the scent gets stronger. I'm surprised up until I slide through the trees at the edge of a waterfall and realize I only catch her because she stopped running.

She's standing on the edge of the waterfall along the wet stone, her back to me, staring down at the churning water far below. Winkie Country is the only Quadrant with a river, and that river doesn't follow any sort of logic. It flows uphill, randomly has waterfalls that shouldn't exist, and when it's feeling feisty, it'll change its course. I'm not sure how Red knew to come here but seeing her standing on the edge of the waterfall sets my nerves on fire. She's too close to the edge. A fall like that might not be easy to recover from. I don't know how easy she is to kill. Will she survive such injuries?

Something warms in my chest, but I ignore it, focusing on her back where claws once scarred her. Seeing them makes me angry at the man who dared to touch her, but I press it down, choosing to think about it later. Right now, I need to get Red away from the edge.

"I don't like this," Ophir whispers in my mind, his worry clear. It's an emotion I haven't felt in a long time and even feeling it secondhand from him is strange.

"What are you doing?" I ask hesitantly, my voice low and calm as if she's a frightened animal.

She looks over her shoulder at me and I see all the memories that haunt her. I've never seen someone look so. . .lost. Tears spill over her lashes, mark her cheeks with their tracks as they drip to the earth below her, adding to the river. She's not in her wolf form, having transformed out if it herself. Progress, and yet she doesn't seem to realize it.

"It's so much darker when a light goes out than it would have been if it had never shone," she rasps.

"So make new light," I growl. It's the wrong thing to say and I know it, but I can't help my nature. Perhaps, it would be better to let Ophir take over. He's always the understanding one.

I take a step toward her, but she doesn't move, hovering just there on the edge of stone. I reach my hand out slowly, offering my clawed fingers for her to take even though she's too far away. She'll have to physically step away from the edge to take my hand. "Come along with me," I murmur.

She stares at my hand, more tears spilling over. "I'm a monster," she breathes. "I can't even control myself."

"There's nothing wrong with being a monster," I reply. "I'm a monster. We all are."

"I don't deserve to walk the earth, not after what I've done. I've killed so many. . ." She chokes on her words and they trail off into nothing.

"*Do something*," Fang growls in my mind.

I'm trying! I shout in my brain. Something else moves in my chest, a crack, but now isn't the time. Anxiety trickles into my body, making me tense.

"The horror you've committed is not who you are," I say, my hand still outstretched toward her. "Control will come with time. I can help you."

I take another step, getting closer in the hopes I can simply grab her away from the edge. I approach her like a spooked animal, knowing at any moment, she can bolt, and I'll never catch her.

Red stares at my hand, watches it, and I see the shift in her eyes.

"*King! Get her!*" Ophir growls in my mind, far rougher sounding than I've ever heard him, but I'm too late.

I move forward another step but without another word, Red meets my eyes. Without uttering a sound, she leans back and falls over the edge of the waterfall.

"Fuck!" I growl and leap after her without a second thought.

The crack in my chest spreads just a little wider. . .

CHAPTER TWENTY-ONE

RED

I'm freefalling.

The wind whips my hair around me like a curtain as I plummet for the churning water below. The moment seems to last forever as I fall, as the violent water draws closer. I only hope it accepts me in its embrace and I can finally be free of the guilt, free of the pain. I can't even function normally, terrified of the smallest things triggering a reaction that kills people. I don't deserve any more chances. Monsters don't deserve a hundred chances.

I slam into the water at the base of the waterfall and sink deep, deeper, until it envelopes me like an old friend. The water is dark and cold, swirling around my skin as the pressure of the water falling above me pushes me deeper, rolling me. I don't fight it. I don't swim. I simply float in the darkness until my lungs burn and true darkness dances along the edge of my eyes.

Staring up at the small beams of light that penetrate, I see the water break again and something shoots through the liquid like an arrow, swimming right for me. Golden eyes fill my gaze before he's wrapping strong arms around my waist and dragging me upwards, away from the darkness, away from the comfort. I don't have the strength to fight, my body limp.

With a violent jerk, I'm thrown from the water onto the bank of the river, my lungs screaming at me until I'm hacking up icy water and gagging on it. I sputter the water out when a large hand smacks my back, forcing more out of my lungs until their clear. Still, they burn as a reminder of what I'd attempted to do.

"What the fuck were you thinking?" he growls. "You could have died!"

With a violent shudder, I begin to sob, collapsing on the ground before him where he kneels soaked through. Once the tears start, I can't stop them, and he freezes at the emotion leaving my lungs, the hopelessness, the fear. I wanted to die. It's better if I die. Then at least I won't kill innocent people. Then I won't be a monster anymore.

Strong hands pick me up so suddenly, I hiccup with the movement. I don't know what I was expecting but it's not the awkward hug King envelopes me in. He's tense, his arms coming around me and gently patting my back. It only makes me cry harder. Here's this emotionless man attempting to comfort me, the monster. After what I'd done.

"We've all done terrible things," he says. "We must live with them. That's our penance."

"Does it ever stop hurting?" I croak through my sobs, pressing myself harder against his warmth.

He goes so still, I worry I've offended him in some way, but when I pull back to look up at him, I realize it isn't King there looking at me. It's Fang.

"No," he answers in his gravel voice. "You just make room for it, little wolf."

My face twists with pain. "You were right. I'm afraid of what I am."

"Fear makes us stronger." He brushes wet hair back from my face. Fang, of the three, is easily the roughest personality. It cracks something wide in me to see him caring, to see tenderness in his words. "You've been scared of love and what it did to you. You're scared of what you've become. But that just means you know which fears to face and where to direct your fierceness."

My fingers clench in his wet shirt, clothing that's only wet because he leapt after me rather than leaving me to die. "Are you afraid?" I ask.

His eyes meet mine and there's profound knowledge there. "I turn my fear into anger, little wolf."

I hiccup and wipe my face on the back of my arm. "I should do the same?"

He shakes his head. "I'm not an example to follow. I am a result. But I will say this. . ."

"Yes?" I ask hesitantly, curling myself against him.

"When robbed of options, you go Feral."

And then King blinks back in control. Only then do I realize how I'm held tenderly in his arms. I expect him to say something, to push me away, but when I press closer, his arms wrap tighter around my shoulders. For once, he's quiet, not having anything else to add to the conversation, but I don't need him to speak. This. This is all I needed. Shivering in the arms of another monster, for the first time in forever, I feel achingly human.

The sound of the waterfall behind us roars in my ears.

CHAPTER TWENTY-TWO

Peter Pan

Aniya and I sit on the edge of the Grimm Forest, both of us staring off into the trees and listening to the sounds of distant banshees. We've been spending more time together since they found me, and I can't say I don't like it. Aniya is a bright young woman, and one day, she'll grow into something greater than either I or her mother ever imagined. She's already greater than all of us.

"Did the arm hurt?" she asks suddenly, staring at the metal that threads into my shoulder.

"Terribly," I admit. "But the pain of building a new arm in its place was worse than losing the appendage to begin with."

My daughter hums in response and tilts her head in a way I've only ever seen the March Hare do. Every day, I thank the hare for being there for Tiger and Aniya when I couldn't. It's clear he loves both of them, and I see the love in Tiger's eyes when she looks back at the Wonderlander. Somehow, I fit into the dynamic. Now that I'm no longer pulled by darkness, I can see things so clearly, can offer more than brutal recklessness.

Just as I can see our dynamic, I can see what the others haven't in

Aniya. They suspect it, sure, but I can feel it. She's a part of me, after all.

"Have you told anyone about the stars?" I murmur, my voice soft to avoid anyone else overhearing us. It's not out of fear they'll accuse me of anything. It's out of fear for my daughter. Power, great power, can frighten people, and sometimes, they react by trying to snuff that power out altogether. I don't think anyone would dare do such a thing to Aniya, but I can never be too sure.

Aniya looks up at me with intelligent eyes. She was so small last I saw her and now she's a young woman. Her powers move around her in a wave that can't be seen, but they're very much felt. My skin cringes away from some of that power, but for the most part, it doesn't effect me.

"Whatever do you mean?" she asks innocently. It could have been seen as mocking, but Aniya isn't like that. She's evaluating how much to say because she doesn't want to worry anyone.

"The stars in your veins," I clarify. "Do they burn? Mine used to burn before I lost the majority of them."

Aniya tilts her head. "They're not lost. They're just no longer tainted by darkness." She blinks. "No. The fire doesn't touch me."

I study her, taking in the galaxies spinning in her eyes. "You're so much more than I ever was."

She smiles. "Yes." No argument. No avoidance. She knows precisely what she is.

"Will you shatter the worlds?" I ask, terrified of her answer. If one day we must face off against our own daughter, I'm not sure us capable of it. I won't ever rise to meet her power.

Her smile widens. "Never."

I breathe a sigh of relief but still I ask, "why not?"

"Because," she shrugs. "All the people I love are here."

And then she goes back to humming as if we'd never spoken of such a profound topic. A banshee screeches in the distance but instead of running toward us, it sounds like it's running away. Somehow, I know it's not me it runs from, but the young woman sitting at my side that carries my blood in her veins.

I don't know much, but I know I dread the day Aniya loses all those she loves.

The worlds will tremble before her. . .

CHAPTER TWENTY-THREE

RED

K ing's castle is small, smaller than the ones I'd seen in Grimm Forest. Just like here, home was filled with rulers, good and bad. My own village had no King over us, but we had a mayor who was often too loose with his ale-drinking. Otherwise, he'd been a decent mayor and never made any passes toward the young women of the village. I'd heard horror stories in other townships and villages. We had nothing like that.

I suppose I became the horror story of my village. . .

Because of the small size of King's castle, it's easy enough to explore until I find myself on the rampart of the structure, my eyes taking in the treetops of the jungle around us. It's impossible to see the entirety of Oz from here—the castle is too short—but from this vantage point, I can see the emerald castle in the distance, just barely glittering with the potential to light up.

At this point, King hasn't told me much about Oz, other than he's an Heir and that there are two others. Then again, I haven't really asked either, too caught up in my own demons to ask for more information. Since we came back from the waterfall and the breakdown I'd had, King has left me to my own devices. I'm almost thankful for it.

I'm not sure if I can look him in the eyes without being reminded of how he held me through my plummet. I'm not sure I can look at him without seeing the images from my dreams and want to act on them.

To the North, or my best guess of it, I can see a glowing city. I can't make out too many details except for the brilliant glow, as if it's lit from within. The buildings are tall and inviting, like metal flowers reaching toward the sky. Intrigue hits me. We didn't have anything like that in the Grimm Forest, not that I'd seen. Familiarity tugs at me but no matter how hard I try, I can't figure out why.

That is how I found myself sitting on the edge of the stone wall, my legs dangling over the edge dangerously, as I stare at the glittering city in the distance. King's domain is nice, beautiful in its poisonous intricacies, but it's different from that sight in the distance. The urge to explore beckons but I'm not sure someone like me should be allowed to do so.

"You must be Scarlett."

The voice startles me, but I don't jump at the sound. It's been ingrained in me too hard to show any sort of weakness. I'm not sure what I expect with the voice when I peer over my shoulder, but it isn't the bubbly woman standing there in a bright blue suit. The outfit is made for her, cutting into her curves savagely and accentuating them. Tiny hearts are stitched into the material, barely a different color so you only see them when she twists in the light. She's beautiful in appearance alone, but her accent when she speaks is just as lively. I've never heard such dialect before.

"Actually, I go by Red," I reply, watching her closely. I'm not sure who she is or where she came from, but she moves far more silently than I expect someone with no powers. As far as I can tell, she smells human, but she's either something I can't detect or she's simply a talented human that can move quietly. I don't know which.

"Awesome," she says, clapping her hands together and stepping forward. "I'm Briella Mae. The boys sent me to hunt for you while they talk about whatever it is they need to talk about."

I tilt my head at her curiously. "It's a pleasure to meet you, Briella Mae."

"Oh," she coos. "Someone else with manners. Was it beaten into you the same way it was me? Mine was an old hag who wanted me to be a debutante and get rid of my roughness, but she didn't succeed." She gestures to herself mockingly though it isn't directed at me. "Obviously."

Blinking, I'm not sure I understand all the words she's spoken. "Umm. . ."

"Never mind that," she continues, waving her words away like she's swatting a bug. Her eyes trail to where I sit with my legs dangling over the edge, dangerously close to falling off. Something flashes in her eyes. Concern? Care? I'm not sure which. "Do I need to worry you'll jump, Red?"

My brows raise at her words, and I look down over the edge to the ground far below. I'd probably survive the fall because of Feral. Still, I have no plans to jump from here and test that theory. Not today.

"No," I answer honestly. "I think I'm okay."

Briella nods. "I just wanted to check. It's best you're always aware of what you're feeling here in Oz. I've learned this world can corrupt your emotions if you're not careful. Even more so when you have a frustrating man trying to control your life."

"Ah," I murmur. "So you have one, too?"

She laughs at my somber tone. "The Tin Man is my. . .boyfriend? That word doesn't really seem to cover what he is. The Hatter uses the word 'mate' for Clara. That feels closer." She meets my eyes with a smile. "Tin is the Heir that rules Gillikin City, just over there." She points out in the distance, toward the glittering city I'd been staring at before she'd arrived.

Briella climbs up hesitantly on the wall beside me and sits down close, her own legs dangling. Though she seems wary of the height, she doesn't shy away from it. A warrior wearing human skin. For long minutes of uninterrupted silence, we simply stare out into the distance, taking in everything before us. The sounds of King's jungle reach my ears, great beasts I can't determine the origin of howling to each other.

"We're here because King asked us to take you to Gillikin with us," Briella murmurs suddenly, glancing over at me. "I'm assuming he didn't inform you of that before we arrived?"

Sadness hits me but I don't show it. Instead, I simply shrug. "He

95

hasn't talked to me about much since. . .well, he hasn't talked to me in a few days now." I bite my lip, hesitating to ask but knowing I'm going to anyways. "Do you know why he's sending me away?"

Briella tilts her head toward me, studying my face. "I'd reckon it's because of the prophesy everyone is talking about. And Toto."

"Prophesy?" King hasn't mentioned any sort of prophesy to me, and I haven't heard the name Toto before. I should have been asking questions, should have wondered, but instead, I was too lost in trying to control Feral to realize things are being hidden. Either it's been on purpose or unconsciously. Either way, it isn't okay. How much do I really know about King? I know his secret but that's about it. He hasn't told me anything else.

"He hasn't told you?" Briella scoffs. "Of course, he hasn't. Arrogant Lion." She shakes her head. "Toto, a powerful lobo, is locked up in Emerald City." She points to the green castle we can see over the tops of the trees. "Once upon a time, he tore his way through Oz, leaving the yellow brick road permanently stained with blood. The Heirs were able to stop him with the help of the Wicked Witch but to do so, they had to lock him up with three locks. Two of the three locks have already been opened, the first one because of me."

"You purposely started releasing him?" I ask, frowning.

Briella shakes her head. "I wouldn't change it now, but I didn't know what I was doing when I asked Rumpelstiltskin to give Tin his heart back. Tink assures me it would have happened regardless if I'd known since that's how prophesies work, but I still feel a little guilty about it." She sighs. "Crow's lock was released in order to save Cinder."

"And how is the third lock going to be released?" I ask. "According to the prophesy?"

"Well, we don't exactly have a paper to follow. But whatever King gave up to lock Toto away has to be returned to him for the lock to break. I don't know what he gave up, but I'm assuming he sees you as a threat to it or else he wouldn't be sending you with us while he stays here."

I roll my eyes at her. "I'm not a threat to him."

"Are you sure about that?" Briella studies me, as if seeing through my answers.

Shrugging, I look away to focus on the glittering city in the distance. I'm not sad I'll be going there but thinking about how King will stay in this castle, locking himself away in fear of breaking the lock, makes me sad.

"He doesn't care about me," I murmur. "In fact, I'm pretty sure I annoy him more than anything."

"I'm pretty sure I annoy Tin every single day," she counters.

"It's different. Clearly, the two of you love each other. That isn't what we have," I argue. It's true, I care for King despite my better senses, but if the opposite were true, he wouldn't be sending me away. Fang probably cares more about me than King does, and he's a gruff asshole.

Briella stares at me for a long moment, searching for whatever it is she thinks she'll find. I don't know if she finds it or not. She schools her expression so well, I barely know what she's thinking at all.

"At every moment in our lives, Red, we've all got one foot in a fairy tale and one foot in the abyss. Be careful you don't fall too far into the darkness convincing yourself that no one cares. There's nothing but pain that way."

I glance up at her, every image of bloodshed I'd caused echoing in my mind. "I don't deserve a fairy tale."

"Then you've already let the darkness win," she replies, standing from her spot and backing away from the edge. "We'll meet you down there when you're ready to go. I've gotta find the little girl's room."

I watch as she walks away, her dark hair bouncing around her shoulders. Even her walk is graceful, as if she once walked down a runway. Envy bites me hard. To be so flawless without trying, it's no wonder the Tin Man fell in love with her. Hell, I'm halfway in love with her myself from our brief interaction. Still, her words echo in my mind.

Then you've already let the darkness win.

I blink against the sudden moisture in my eyes, keeping it at bay. I can't afford to cry, not right now.

In my chest, Feral shifts and curls around me in comfort, and for the first time since we became one, I pull her closer.

CHAPTER TWENTY-FOUR

OPHIR

King has receded in our mind, shoving me forward to take precedence. It's strange. Not once in my memory can I remember King relinquishing control so willingly. Not ever. And yet here he is, giving me free reign, retreating so deep, I can barely sense him in the background. I don't think he's even listening in on our conversation. Of course, he would leave me to explain things to Crow and Tin. Acting like King is nearly impossible for me, but I try my hardest to appear stern and abrasive before the two other Heirs walk inside the castle.

I haven't seen Red in a few days, King doing his best to avoid her presence, and I despise him for it. Since the waterfall incident, he'd distanced himself from her, choosing to ignore the problem and send her away rather than face it head on. He's trying to hide from what's happening, but Fang and I can see it, can feel it.

There's a crack in our consciousness, and there's only one thing that can cause that.

"Fill it up," Fang grunts in my mind. *"If Toto gets out—"*

"There's no way to fill a crack when that crack is magic," I argue. "It's prophesied to happen anyways—"

"*Yes, but no one is prepared. All it'll take is one little accident and he'll be released. It's the woman. She's the threat.*" Fang's voice turns into a growl in my mind, sending my hackles rising as if he's in control. Still, he doesn't actually take control. Fang prefers to remain silent and back most of the time. Only recently has he started coming forward more.

"It's not her fault," I counter. "She's done nothing wrong."

"*She's broken,*" Fang snarls. "*Her brokenness begs for empathy.*"

I go silent at his response, at the words he'd found the audacity to utter, even if they're inside our mind. They're harsh words, cruel even, and I'm surprised that I'm surprised at Fang's attitude at all. He always was the harsher one between the three of us. The words are not so far off his mark.

"*What?*" Fang hisses. "*Nothing to say to that?*"

Moving over to the mirror in the room, I stare into my reflection, seeing both my face and Fang's when he speaks. Right now, it's my kinder eyes peering back at me, showing precisely how I feel.

"If you see a broken woman, then you're not seeing her at all," I say, my voice loud in the room. "King is hiding from it, afraid of what caring will do, but I'm no coward despite the rumors." I stare into my reflection, into our eyes. "Red is a wolf, and a wolf will never be a pet. We should know that."

Fang's eyes narrow in the mirror, glaring at me. He's angry, sure, but there's also confusion there. Something like this is far outside Fang's realm of understanding. He cares for Red in his own way, but I'm not sure the third of our triad will know care if it smacked him in the face.

"*But Toto—*"

"Is inevitable," I interrupt. "And if King continues to run from it, if you do, then you're both the cowards they say we are."

Without another word, Fang disappears in the mirror just as Tin, Crow, and Briella enter the front door, their eyes searching around until they find me. Of course, Fang would shy away from this. Of course, him and King would disappear and leave me to deal with things.

Briella immediately nods her head to me and gestures toward the staircase in question.

Nodding, I say, "I believe she's on the roof."

"I'll go find her," Briella says, immediately leaving the three of us to talk.

"Welcome to my home," I tell Tin and Crow, bowing my head just barely, forgetting for a moment that it should be King speaking. I'm reminded of that fact when Tin pauses and frowns, his head tilting toward me.

"What's wrong with you? Why are you talking like that?"

I pause, trying to rearrange my mannerisms to be those like King, but I'm not the arrogant asshole he is. I've never been. Still, I try my best.

"I don't know what you mean but we have a situation," I reply gruffly, crossing my arms for emphasis. King always likes to show off his forearm muscles.

"Right. You said you need the woman out of your realm," Tin replies, his eyes still narrowed in suspicion. "Briella will keep her company until we do so."

Crow stares at me. "Your lock?" he finally asks.

"Still intact," I surmise. "For now. But if there was ever someone who can break it, it's her."

Tin takes a step closer, frowning. "And you openly admit that?"

I curse King's ability to hide any sort of weakness in a way that makes this conversation appear strange to Tin. I'm only trying to help matters, to clarify what's happening. I try and shove my own feelings away, ones I very much feel. It was only King who gave up his empathy. Though Fang is less capable of it, both he and I still feel stronger than King can with the lock in place.

"There's a crack already," I admit, meeting Tin's eyes. "I don't know how it'll be broken completely, but I figure it best to ask for help before we're caught unprepared."

Crow leans against the bookshelf full of war tomes and battle strategies. I dislike the books myself, but both King and Fang enjoy them. I much preferred tales of heroic feats.

"You sound like you expect it to break regardless," Crow murmurs, studying me closely. "How long do we have?"

"That, I don't know," I admit. "But I believe it's time to prepare."

"For what exactly?" Tin asks, crossing his arms in a mimicry of my position, his eyes hard.

"War." He already knows that, but I get the feeling he's testing me in some way, getting me to talk more so he can figure out what's different. Problem is, neither of them will ever expect exactly what I am. "I'll come with you to Gillikin when you go."

I move to pass Tin, knowing I'll need to prepare for leaving. Tin stops me with a hand on my chest before I can pass, his gaze strong and threatening. Suspicion fills his eyes.

"You said you wanted us to take her with us, *away* from you," Tin adds. "Why the sudden change of heart?"

Meeting his eyes, I allow him to see deeper, confusing him even more. "Because I'm in charge of this body, and so that's what I have decided."

Tin's face twists. "What an odd way to phrase that."

Crow is still staring at me, at the interaction between the Tin Man and me. "What did you give up?" he finally asks when we don't move. "That day. What is your lock?"

"My empathy," I hum.

"So it should be impossible for you to care right now," he replies, but Tin is shaking his head.

"It's not. Not impossible. I shouldn't have been able to love Briella before my lock broke, and yet, I knew I could love her before my heart was returned. I felt it, like a muted down promise."

Absorbing his words, I nod. That must be how King is still developing feelings despite the lock. "That's precisely what it feels like."

Crow's eyes widen, and I realize he probably doesn't understand because his soul had been an external thing. Just because he hadn't held his soul didn't mean that he couldn't love. He just had a harsher take on things before. Now, he saved Cinder with that very soul, giving it up for her rather than taking it back within himself. It would be beautiful if he hadn't had to destroy a friend in the process.

"We should prepare—" Crow begins, but the door slams open before he can finish and all three of us turn toward the doorway.

Red stands there alone in all her furious glory, her hair flared wide at her bold movements. "You're sending me away?" she growls, the threat in those words.

Both Tin and Crow step back, and though I tense, I don't back down.

I won't be a coward.

CHAPTER TWENTY-FIVE

RED

"You promised you'd help me control it!" I snarl, stepping further inside the room. I completely ignore the other two men standing around, my eyes on the man determined to send me away. How dare he after everything we talked about?

"Red—" he starts to say but I cut him off, too angry to listen to an excuse.

"How dare you send me away like this! You're nothing but a coward!"

"I'm going with you," he says quickly, attempting to get the words out before I interrupt him again, but all that does is make me freeze in realization.

This isn't King at all. Though someone else might not be able to tell the difference, I've figured out the small nuances between their voices. Ophir is always softer spoken though strong. King is abrasive and emotionless. Fang is all gruff restrained anger. The man in front of me is Ophir. King isn't speaking.

"Where is he?" I growl, storming forward. I see one of the other men frown, the one I assume is the Tin Man. There's metal along his face, catching in the light of the room. "I want to talk to him."

"He's receded," Ophir admits.

"Tell him I have a bone to pick with him," I say, moving closer, my fury needing someone to direct it at. My problem isn't with Ophir. After all, he changed the plan so that he's coming with me, but King is still hiding away.

"He won't listen."

"Make him listen!" My voice is gravel on its own, revealing the wolf inside me slowly unfurling in my anger. I'm sure my eyes are glowing, but I don't care to stop them.

"What the fuck is going on?" the Scarecrow asks, his face twisted in angry confusion. "Who are you talking about?"

But I ignore him in favor of the Lion before me. "Ophir, tell him now."

"I've tried," Ophir says, opening his hands as if to show me. "He's afraid of the lock breaking."

"And Fang?" I ask.

"The same."

I laugh but there's no humor in the sound. I'm hurt by their reaction, the avoidance of dealing with me. I know I'm not that important to King, but I'd at least hoped Fang cared. I'd felt his care, I thought. "Of course," I murmur, staring at Ophir for a moment. When the idea enters my mind, I already regret it, but if I have to do it in order to get King to speak to me, I will. Still, I don't want to hurt Ophir. "I'm sorry, Ophir."

"For what?" he asks, watching me carefully.

"For this."

The knife is flicked out from the halfway rope I'd tied around my thigh to hold it the next second. King hasn't given me any other clothing other than his shirts, so I've been left at a disadvantage. When I'd taken the knife from dinner, I wasn't sure if I would ever need to use it. I don't want to shift just yet in order to hurt him, don't want to reveal my hand. Pain should make King come out. I'm sure of it. He won't stand for constant pain.

Without waiting for an answer, I stab the knife deep into Ophir's shoulder and jerk it out, drawing blood among his other scars. He grunts and slaps a clawed hand over the wound, holding up his other hand toward Tin and Crow to stop them from grabbing me. I back away from them just in case.

"Don't hurt her," Ophir orders the other Heirs.

"She's just stabbed you!" Tin says, his face twisting in confusion. "I didn't realize you were into such things."

"She's trying to help," Ophir argues.

Crow stops and shakes his head. "This is fucking ridiculous. We need answers right now."

I dart in again when no one grabs me. "Talk to me, you coward!" I shout, stabbing the knife in on the opposite shoulder. He'll heal quickly but, despite that, he'll still feel the pain.

"Stop stabbing him!" Tin growls. "That's not helping matters!"

The door slams open again, Briella Mae standing there with an axe in her hand. "What the fuck is going on?" she yells, her eyes wide in panic. When she sees the knife in my hand and the wounds on who she thinks is King, she lowers the axe, her brows going up. "What did he do?"

I launch at Ophir again, determined to force King out if I have to keep stabbing his body. I scream in fury as I launch at him, desperate to talk, but this time, Ophir doesn't just let me land a blow. A clawed hand wraps around my wrist and stops me from embedding the knife into his shoulder again. The atmosphere in the room changes, as if everyone can sense something is different but not understanding what.

"You're a coward," I growl up into King's face, my own twisted in anger.

King's face is emotionless in the face of my fury, but he doesn't release my wrist where I push harder to stab him. "I don't care what you think of me."

"That's right. You don't care for anything at all, do you?" I spit.

His eyes clash with minc, the gold of his lion meeting the gold of my wolf. "No." One word holding all the answers.

"So you just break your promise to help me because you're afraid."

"I'm not afraid."

"Liar," I accuse. Without waiting for another reply, I drop the knife from the wrist he holds and catch it with the other. I slam it to the hilt into his side. King grunts in pain but he doesn't avoid the hit.

With so much emotion filling my body, I'm not surprised when my bones begin to pop. My legs begin to lengthen slowly, my fingers lengthening into claws. Something pops in my face, and I hear Briella gasp from behind me.

"Whoa!" she says, and I can feel her surprise. Did King not tell them what I am?

Tin shoves the human woman behind him but she peeks out from where he protects her, her eyes wide.

"Stop it," King growls.

"Or what?" I snarl, my voice thick with Feral as she asks for permission to take over. Still, I slow the transformation, not wanting to change but wanting to prove a point. "You going to kill me, Lion?"

"Don't push me, little wolf." His eyes are hard, threatening, but I'm not afraid of monsters. I haven't been afraid of monsters since I became one.

Without waiting for him to move, I shove the bloody knife into his own hand, forcing him to take it, making his fingers curl around the hilt.

"Then do it, you coward! Kill me." He doesn't move, his eyes jumping between the knife in his hand and my eyes. "Kill the monster who can't control herself!"

Crow is holding his hand out to me as if that'll ease Feral if she wants to attack him, but she's not fighting to massacre the room. She's fighting to comfort me, feeling my turmoil inside.

I wrap my hand around King's, around the one with a knife and jerk it forward toward my chest, not piercing but close enough to doing so if I move. "Go on. Do it." My face hardens. "And when you kill the monster, make sure you say her name." I jerk him forward, or try to, but he holds strong, the knife tip just out of reach, his hands keeping the steel from ever meeting my skin.

We're staring at each other as if it's a face off. My bones continue to lengthen and shorten, popping in and out of transformation, not because I can't control it, but because we can't decide which form is better for this. I don't want to change into her, knowing it's a mistake, but with so many emotions filling me, it's a way to expel some of the energy. Though the bones cause me pain, I'm hardly focused on it. Instead, I wait for King to make a decision.

His hand spasms in front of me and he drops the knife, letting it clatter to the ground. Blood, his blood, splatters around it, bright red against the dark wood.

I chuckle darkly at him, sinister, hurt. "That's what I thought," I rasp. "You're nothing but a coward."

I jerk out of his hold and turn, prepared to walk away. I'm going with Briella and the others because, clearly, there's no reason to stay. King won't admit he cares, can barely look at me as anything other than a nuisance. Why stay with someone who won't return the feelings I've been battling since I stormed through the jungle to find him?

My bones pop back to human, making my few steps jerky as they take a moment to go back to normal, but before I can leave, thick claws wrap around my wrist and jerk me back around to face King. He's staring down at me, his expression fierce, his eyes glowing with. . .is that emotion?

"I'm no coward," he snarls savagely.

And then without waiting a second longer, he slams his lips against mine.

CHAPTER TWENTY-SIX

BRIELLA MAE

"This is not where I was expecting things to go," I whisper from behind Tin, my eyes wide. "I don't know if this is romantic or wild. Maybe it's wildly romantic. Maybe I've lost my damn mind being in Oz."

Tin laughs at my words but he still keeps me behind him as if afraid Red will attack us. Silly man. Red has more control of herself than everyone thinks. She might not have been able to control whatever she is before, but she clearly can now. I'm not even certain what she is but there's something familiar about the small changes that had taken hold before shrinking away. Now, she stands completely human, dressed in a masculine, torn shirt. Girl needs some new clothing. My mind already starts to think up designs for her.

"We should get out of here," Crow murmurs. "They clearly have things to. . .discuss."

I can't stop myself from doing a little dance behind Tin and against him, making him look over his shoulder at me in confusion.

"What on Oz are you doing?" he asks, frowning until he sees me. He can't help but smile at my dorkiness despite him being the big bad Tin Man.

"Bow chicka wow wow!" I purr while simultaneously gyrating against Tin's backside.

He snorts but doesn't move, uncaring that Crow is watching in amusement.

At my words and movement, Red breaks the kiss between the two and looks me, her face crimson to match her name. I'm almost tempted to laugh at her embarrassment, but before I can tease her about King clearly "not caring" about her, the temperature in the room drops so drastically, I can see my breath.

"Wait. What's happening?" I ask, confused even as I press against Tin to steal his warmth.

But Tin isn't looking at me. His eyes are on King where he stands before Red. King still has his claws settled on Red's waist, but his eyes are glazed over, as if he isn't seeing her as much as looking within himself.

"King?" Red asks, noticing his look.

And that's when all Hell breaks loose.

Back home, just before it rains, you smell it first, and then you feel it in the air, almost like an electrical charge that sets your hairs on end. That's exactly what happens to the air inside the small room we stand in.

One second, we're all staring at King curiously. The next, a blast of energy shoves us all back and King's back bows so violently, I hear it crack with strain. A shout of agony splits his lips as something bright slams into his chest, lighting him up like a Christmas tree.

"What the fuck?!" I shout even a Tin presses me back against the wall. I couldn't have moved if I wanted to, not with the energy slamming repeatedly into us. "What's happening?"

I watch as Red fights the force pushing us back and tries to drag her way back toward King and his pain. Her fingers are sharpened to claws she digs into the wood of the floor, shattering it in each place where they sink in. Still, she struggles to reach him, fighting as hard as she can. I can see her strain and know I could never fight against it. I'm still human, despite feeling a little stronger each day.

Crow doesn't even fight against being pressed into the wall. Instead, his expression is sad as he stares at King. He sighs as King's shout of pain gets more anguished. "The third lock," he breathes, and despite the swirling wind and power, we can still hear him.

Tin curses. "We're not ready. We need to get back to Gillikin."

"It doesn't matter if we're ready," Crow answers, and I feel the weight of his next words. "The choice has been made for us."

Red starts to scream as she fights against the power stabbing into her skin.

CHAPTER TWENTY-SEVEN

KING

I ntense pain slams into my body and fills my veins. It feels like both fire and ice, as if I'm burning alive and freezing solid at the same time. Everything in my body violently reacts against the sudden intrusion. The enemy isn't one I can fight, so I don't even try, understanding all too well what's happening without having to hear anyone else confirm it.

The third lock is being broken. All because I care for the woman desperately attempting to reach me from across the room.

"*She's afraid for us,*" Ophir grunts, the pain effecting more than me. All three of us are in pain. All three feel the weight of prophesy.

"*Is she okay?*" Fang's voice, worried.

I don't answer. I can't. Every time I open my mouth, an agonized yell comes out. I can't control the pain, can't fight against it. I never expected it to feel like this when my empathy was returned. Had it hurt Tin and Crow just as much? Or am I the unlucky fool that gets the pain because my lock is last?

There's a sound like a crack of lightning and the side of my castle is blown wide, letting in the sight of my jungle and Emerald City in the distance. Where it once was a dull green, the castle is lit up like a beacon. Oz shakes beneath my feet, and I feel the moment the lock completely breaks and my empathy that I once gave up slams right back into my chest like an axe.

Memories slam back inside me, moments where I should have felt but couldn't. Fang and Ophir shrink back inside my mind, having already witnessed the moments through my eyes, but the pain is just as strong for them. I bear the burden of the true pain myself, protecting them from it as best as I can, only because it's my fault this is happening.

The memories had been muted once, but now they come back full force.

The moment Azalea lay injured in my arms after having given up nearly everything to lock Toto away inside his makeshift prison.

The realization that Tin's lock had broken and started the chain reaction for where we're at now.

When Crow gave up his soul for Cinder, breaking the lock but saving the woman he loves.

The first time I saw Red come sliding around the corner in town, her eyes meeting mine and something inside of me waking up at her appearance.

Seeing her fall over the waterfall. . .

Each emotion is replaced with the proper one, and for the first time in so long, I feel.

I *feel.*

It's as if a needle is stabbed inside my brain and then travels throughout my body.

And then everything stops.

The world quiets. The wind releases and disappears. The air stills.

A long, *angry* howl cuts the air around us.

Red stands before me, fully human with bleeding fingertips where she'd fought to get closer, her eyes wide and terrified.

"I'm sorry," she whispers, and then she's taking off through the shattered wall of the castle and disappearing into the trees.

CHAPTER TWENTY-EIGHT

RUMPELSTILTSKIN

I stand on the edge of Quadling Country and Emerald City, watching as Ananke hovers before me. There's a phantom wind around her, gently swirling her blonde hair and giving her an eerie appearance. Even if she wasn't as powerful as she is, even if she wasn't a World Breaker, Ananke would feel unnatural and I don't know why that is.

Perhaps, it's because she feels as if she's no longer whole.

From the other side of the line, Toto appears, a great hulking creature that once sent Oz into chaos. Dorothy had let him in, or so I've been told, but he'd chosen to stay and destroy. Apparently, Dorothy had been the first casualty. This beast has no loyalty, will never have loyalty, but his eyes focus on the beauty before me as if she set the world in motion. Power calls to power, and though Toto is powerful on his own, he's not as powerful as Ananke. For that reason alone, he'll follow her into war.

Toto hesitates on the other side of the boundary, a line he hadn't been able to cross before. Now, he hovers there, feeling that he's free but uncertain if he truly is. Perhaps, he doesn't quite believe it. Not yet.

When Ananke offers her hand to him, outstretched in a way that can only be seen as an invitation, he takes another hesitant step forward. In order to take her hand, he'll have to cross completely.

I've never seen the beast in his human form, and he doesn't change now. He chooses to remain the monster over anything else, to hold himself taller than most. His glowing eyes would give me chills if I wasn't doing my best to school my features and draw his attention.

After all, he has no loyalty to me.

With a final breath, Toto steps across the boundary and slips his claws into Ananke's. He sighs in contentment and the insane woman I've found myself following reaches up to caress his face like he's no more than a puppy. I feel his power reach out and brush against me, making my already overstimulated skin cringe.

"And so it begins," she purrs up to him, and he grins in answer.

A shiver runs through me, and I know, without a doubt, I have to get away from them and out of Oz.

My very life depends on it. . .

CHAPTER TWENTY-NINE

RED

P ure panic fills me. I've doomed Oz, released the danger, instead of just leaving like King had wanted and saving them all. I'm selfish, only thinking of myself rather than this world trying desperately to survive. I've started a war.

Feral stays at bay and I find myself running through the jungle completely human. Though I'm panicked and full of emotion, the transformation doesn't come, as though she knows I can't handle the wildness right now. Even if I change, I won't hurt anything that doesn't get in my way. I'm just trying to get away, to run from my problems. How can I face him again knowing what I'd instigated?

I just hadn't wanted King to send me away.

A sob chokes in my throat and I stumble in my panicked run, just barely catching myself before I fall. My bare feet slice open as I sprint across the ground, putting distance between me and the castle behind me. This isn't what I had in mind. I'm clinging to King despite him wanting nothing to do with me. Why am I putting this world in danger?

Even with everything, King has somehow helped me. I'm in control of Feral, have accepted her without even realizing it. When had that happened? At what point had I stopped looking at Feral as a monster and started thinking of her as kin? It's easier to hold the reins now.

In the distance, I hear King call my name, hear him give chase, but how can I face him after what I've done?

I push myself harder, but even with how hard I push my human legs, I know it's not enough. I feel the presence of a predator before I know it's him, and my panic increases. I can't face him. I have to get out of here. I have to escape and live with what I've done.

Something snaps behind me, but I don't turn around. I can't outrun this predator. I know I can't. With my panic ruling my body, I break through the tree line into a small clearing and slide to a stop, turning to face him. I can smell him, can sense him, but when I think he's going to break through the dark trees, he doesn't. All sound halts as he stays just out of sight. The atmosphere has me crouching, preparing for an attack that might never come. I don't know what he has planned, but I know I won't go down without a fight if he's here to kill me after all. Feral won't allow me to. Not anymore.

"I can smell you," I say into the silence jungle.

The plant life moves around, looking for a meal, but they don't give away their King, don't point in his direction.

"Show yourself," I growl, annoyed at my body's reaction to this cat and mouse game.

"Little wolf, little wolf, let me in." The voice comes from the darkness, but I can't see him. I turn in the direction of the voice, searching, only to find more darkness.

"Games are for children," I call, my fingers lengthening into claws out of instinct. I can't help the desire that pools in my belly at the game, can't help the sudden arousal as his own claws drag down the bark of a tree in the darkness before he dances away, as silent as a jungle cat.

"What sharp claws you have, little wolf," he purrs, and I can hear Fang in that voice, know it's him talking to me. I turn in the direction knowing he's already gone. "Show me your claws."

"Come here and I'll show you," I breathe, my voice husky.

The voice comes from directly behind me. "Show me your fangs."

I can't turn, my body suddenly frozen by the large, beautiful arm that snakes around me, his claws wrapping around the front of my neck and turning my head to the side. He pins my back against his front, holding me still. His other claws settle on my hip, pressing gently there despite the threat hanging in the air between us.

"Do you fear my monster, little wolf?" he asks huskily.

"No," I breathe. "But Fang—"

"Shh," he murmurs. "Don't waste your time apologizing."

"But I—"

"Now, who's the coward?" he goads. He leans closer, his breath caressing my ear, and whispers, "little wolf, little wolf, let me in."

His body heat is against my back, soaking into me, stroking the fire already burning higher. His hand remains around my throat and my core tenses dangerously. My back arches of its own accord, and before my brain notices the agreement, my body has already made the decision.

"Okay," I rasp.

A husky chuckle is my reward. "Good girl."

And then the claws at my hip slip beneath the shirt I wear and touches my burning flesh.

CHAPTER THIRTY

Telling the three personalities apart is almost as easy as breathing now. I don't know why it's so easy for me to tell when Fang takes over when I can't even see his face, but I know without a doubt that's who growls in my ear. I know that's who holds me.

"There's no running from this." His voice is thick with arousal. "You were meant to be mine."

"Maybe it's *you* who were meant to be mine," I counter, my voice breathy as his fingers trace along my nipple, teasing with his claws.

I expect him to argue, maybe growl about how I belong to him and nothing else. The masculinity I've encountered throughout my life has always been fragile. I shouldn't have lumped them into the same category though.

"Yes," he purrs, and I can feel his length pressing against my backside, a promise of what's to come. "We belong to each other."

His teeth scrap against my neck, sending a shiver through my body, but despite my arousal, guilt still tugs at my soul.

"You don't hate me?"

He pauses against me, and then with claws that I should be afraid of, he tears the shirt I'm wearing down the middle, leaving it to gap wide. The jungle around us is alive with the sounds of creatures but none of them dare come around the king. Even the plants stay away, leaving us to our own devices. The sound of the fabric ripping makes me jump against him despite his other hand holding my throat in a vice.

"Silly wolf," he growls against my skin. "I could never hate you, not even in the beginning when I desperately wanted to. We are yours just as you are ours."

With a jerk, he pulls the loose material from my shoulders, dropping it to the ground. Fang doesn't let me take control, but I don't expect him to. When he turns me and presses me back against the bark of the nearest tree, I have a moment of worry the tree will take advantage. It doesn't move, as if the Lion being so close is all it takes to make it act as all trees should. Fang caresses my jaw just before he presses harsh lips against mine. Earlier, when King had been in control, the kiss had been forceful but restrained. With Fang, there isn't an ounce of restraint. His tongue immediately dances inside to tangle with mine, his hand on my jaw directing me how he wants me to move. Every so often, I can feel the sharp bite of his teeth against my lip, practically asking my own teeth to sharpen, but I hold Feral at bay. I want to be present for this, to be completely here.

Fang pulls back and meets my eyes, his golden eye and cloudy eye meeting mine straight on, staring into my soul. They burn brightly despite one being bisected with a scar and I can feel his desire to eat me whole. That thought has my body writhing against him.

"I'm going to keep you on the edge," he promises, his eyes fierce with wildfire. "I'm going to wring pleasure from you until you beg me to push you over the fucking cliff."

I clamp my thighs together at his words, my body practically melting at his words. I've always known the Lion is sexy but seeing him here with the intent to destroy me. . .for the first time ever, I won't mind my destruction. Perhaps, I don't need a blade to end me. Perhaps, all it takes is a determined Lion and his claws.

Still fully clothed, he leans down to press his lips against my chest, trailing his tongue down, down, down, until he's kneeling before me.

When the mighty Lion, King of Winkie Country, Heir of Oz, looks up at me with fierce eyes, something inside me moves in satisfaction. This man kneels for no one, but here he sits prone on his knees for me. Carefully, I reach forward and thread my fingers through his hair and I swear the big, tough Lion purrs at my touch. I don't have long to appreciate it, however. With a hum of mischief, Fang hooks my leg behind the knee and tosses it over his muscled shoulder. Without giving me a chance to understand what's about to happen, his lips are already at my core, his tongue sweeping up my seam with a long pull.

My head goes back automatically, and I nearly slam it into the tree I lean against for balance. "Oh," I moan, holding him against me. His claws stroke up my thighs, along my hip, carving tiny lines that'll be gone within the hour. When his tongue swirls against my clit, I think my eyes roll back in my head.

He leans back, just a little, and it takes everything in me not to shove him back between my legs. Only the fear of being selfish and greedy stalls my hand. Only the guilt of what I've already taken from him keeps me from fighting for control.

"You taste like fire and the wild," he growls. His teeth nip my inner thigh, likely leaving a mark but I don't care. I just want him to keep going, to torture me some more.

"Show me," I beg, tugging gently on his hair, and the answering smile that curls his lips makes my insides flip.

When he presses his lips against me again, my body tenses, climbing to the edge he promised, rolling with waves of pleasure. He sucks hard against my bundle of nerves, tugging, and before I know what's happening, I'm falling off the cliff, diving off it really. I could have no more stopped it than I can fly. My legs shake with the release, nearly making me buckle if not for the tree bracing my back and Fang holding my thighs.

Fang slows his ministrations, gently nibbling at me before pulling back to look up at me. "Was that to your liking, little wolf?"

Slowly, looking at him through half-lidded eyes, I nod, content.

"Good. Because we're not finished."

Still kneeling before me, he pulls his shirt over his head and tosses it away. His muscles all stand gloriously on display, and I find myself caressing along his strong shoulders, trailing my fingers along the divots and definition. How beautiful he is. When Oz made the Heirs, it certainly made them in some sort of image, although I doubt anything could compare to what the Lion is. Someone like him isn't meant to be anything other than glorious.

While I stare at him and admire his beauty, he does the same to me, his hands trailing along my body. As his hands trace a path for his lips to follow, I stand there, not sure what to do, not sure if my legs will be strong enough to do much more than keep my body upright.

Fang lifts me off my feet for a brief second before he's tugging me down to his level, rolling us backward and over until I'm beneath him on the leaf-covered ground. The gruffest of the three stares at me as if I'm something worth staring at, as if I'm more than a monster desperate for redemption.

"No more running," he says. "Not from us."

I hesitate. Can I promise something like that? My instinct, when I'm afraid or anxious or overwhelmed, is to separate from the situation. I'd felt immeasurable guilt when the third lock broke—another problem that needs to be addressed—and my instinct was to run from it rather than see the blame in King's eyes. But he isn't blaming me now. He isn't condemning me.

"Promise me," Fang growls, his eyes tracing over my face. "Or no more pleasure for you."

"You'd blackmail me?" I ask, narrowing my eyes. "Just to get your way?"

"Did you expect anything other than a monster, little wolf?" he asks, a saccharine smile tugging at his lips. "This is not a pairing between two humans. We're beasts, and like beasts, we shall act."

Biting my lip, I run my hands along his biceps as he holds himself over me. "To be a beast would not be so bad, as long as I'm beastly with you."

Fang nods and leans down to press a kiss right in the center of my chest. "No more running," he repeats.

"No more running," I promise, before a grin bares my own teeth. "Unless I simply want you to chase me."

A husky chuckle breaks his smile and then his hands are caressing along my body again. "Ophir is begging for an appearance," Fang admits, looking up into my eyes. "Should I allow him to pleasure you sweetly?"

My breath hitches and I'm nodding before I fully know the answer. Clearly, my body knows what it's doing. The Lion isn't only one; he's three. To expect anything less than to love all three of them would be foolish, but something in my mind wants all three of them to love me in return. Is love possible? Will I even recognize it once it's there? I hadn't loved Perry, but this is different.

Do we even have to love each other to be prophesied as one?

"You're thinking awfully hard, Scarlett," Ophir murmurs, kind eyes looking down at me. He settles himself between my thighs, his hips pressing against me. Though he's aroused, he doesn't pressure me into moving. Instead, he gently tucks hair away from my face and waits for me to come back from my thinking.

"I'm just wondering how prophesies work," I admit, reaching up to press my hand against his chest, right over the claw marks I'd left upon our first meeting. They're healed now, but white lines still scar the skin, a mark left behind as a reminder of me.

"Ah, a most difficult and yet easy topic," he says, grinding his hips against mine and drawing a gasp from my lips. "You see, prophesies can be as large as to encompass an entire world, or so small, it effects a single person."

Ophir reaches down and unfastens the ties of his pants, freeing his length to my eyes. I can't help but look down between us to admire him, to take in the build. Everything about him is perfect, as if he'd been sculpted by an artist. Perhaps he had been. I don't know how Oz creation works.

If only I were so lovingly sculpted.

"The prophesy that brought us together encompasses a world, the three Heirs and their mates destined to fall into their lives. Some of us, literally." He smiles. "Naturally, you charged into ours determined to rip us to shreds."

I tilt my head at him, studying his eyes, still amazed that, despite them wearing the same face, each is as different as if they are different people. Their expressions, their voices, their mannerisms, are all completely separate somehow.

"You've never shown me your beast," I comment.

He pauses at my words, as if he hadn't expected them. "Would it surprise you to know none of Oz have witnessed my beast?"

"Yes." I cup his face with both of my hands. "You, who preached to me about accepting my own beast, hides your own away from the world."

His length nudges at my entrance, a welcome distraction. Before he presses inside me, he looks down at me. "Perhaps, if there was ever anyone I would show who I really am to, it will be you, Scarlett."

And then he's inside me, my wetness making the movement easy. Where I knew Fang would have brutally taken me for a ride, Ophir is a careful lover. He strokes inside me with long, powerful strokes, slowly pushing my desire higher and higher.

"Beautiful," he groans as he looks down at me, as he holds himself tense so as not to crush me, but I'm not some delicate flower.

With fingers tipped with claws, I wrap my arms around his ribs and jerk him down until his weight covers me. I don't wait for him to chastise me. Instead, I spear my hand into his hair and jerk his mouth to mine, kissing him with a furious desire to consume him completely. Ophir and Fang claim they belong to me, and so I will give them everything that I am.

Ophir groans against my lips and strokes inside me harder, rocking me against the ground, driving me so high, I think I'll never fall off the cliff, perched there as if waiting.

"Come for me," he commands against my lips, my generous lover finding his assertiveness.

As if that's precisely what I was waiting for, I tumble over the ledge with a cry of pleasure, my body undulating beneath him.

"Again," he groans, not slowing his pace. Instead, he picks up his speed. "Red."

I know it's King who speaks when I open my eyes and see him looking down at me. Where there had been no emotion before, care splits his face, his eyes fierce as they look down upon me. I need him desperately, the one personality of the three I thought would always hate me.

His eyes flash gold and I pause for a moment, fighting everything inside me that wants to run. Instincts beg me to run, not because I'm afraid of the man over me, but because I want him to chase me. I want him to catch me.

"You promised," he reminds me, as if he knows exactly what I'm thinking about.

"My instincts are difficult to fight. I've seen so many look at me with fear, with anger, that I expected the same thing from you when the lock broke," I whisper, looking away.

Strong fingers caress my chin and drag my gaze back to his. "It's hard to let go of your demons, isn't it?" he murmurs, holding me still. He's still nestled inside me, his hard length unmoving while we speaks. I shift beneath him and he smiles before he obliges me and moves with tiny, torturous movements.

"They held me when no one else would," I answer, knowing what he's asking. My demons still haunt my nightmares, still haunt my day. Sometimes, the nightmares follow me when I wake and appear before my eyes, covering the reality before me. My demons, my Feral, have allowed me to fight them, have given me the tools to do so. Trauma is a hell of a drug when you've lived with it for so long.

King nods. "I understand." He leans down. "But now, we're here to hold you instead."

I blink up at him, at the adoration in his gaze I never expected to see. Moisture gathers at the corner of my eyes at his words, surprised by what he's saying.

"Do you mean that?" I ask, my palm pressing against his jaw. I want so desperately to mean something to this man, to have him by my side as we fight whatever threat is coming to the world. It's time I find a way to accept my beast completely, to encourage Feral to be a permanent part of me as she's meant to be. I'm not a victim. I'm a survivor, and though I should have never been forced to be a survivor, I was strong long before Perry came and fucked up my life. I can be both strong and savage, both beastly and good.

"We do," King replies, seeing the moment in my eyes I decide the monster I'm going to be.

I pull him in for another kiss and let the Lion love me until I forget for a moment the danger we've just released into the world, all because we couldn't resist each other.

Sometimes, destiny isn't to be trifled with.

Sometimes, she wins, and we're all the better for it.

CHAPTER THIRTY-ONE

TIN MAN

"We don't have time for this," I growl, staring off into the trees. There's no question about what's happening out in the jungle right this very moment between King and Red. I'd seen King's face as he'd chased after his woman. I probably would have done the same if the situation were reversed, and had done so in my time, but King doesn't have the same luxury that Crow and I had. There's no down time between the lock breaking and war. The third lock is broken, and Toto is free. Who knows what he's already getting up to? "We need to get back to Gillikin now and rally the others."

I can't help the sudden urge to start pacing. Crow watches me carefully. Briella stands to the side with her arms crossed, perfectly content to give the new lovebirds their time. As she'd reminded me, it's better for everyone to have whatever they needed said spoken before we march into war. I can't blame her reasoning. If I could protect Briella Mae from the war coming, I'd have caged her away. The silly woman would find her way out and end up protecting me. I'm smart enough to know it will be foolish to cage her. She'll only escape.

"They won't attack right away," Crow reminds me, his logic

annoying me. "Toto isn't in charge so, though he may want to raze Oz to the ground, he'll wait for her orders. She will have a plan that she wants to enact rather than march in and risk losing."

"I have to prepare," I grunt, shoving a hand through my hair and tousling it the same way Briella's hands do. When I mess it up, her eyes brighten, always liking the way it looks.

"I'm anxious to get back, too," Crow reminds me. "My soul is there."

I soften at the mention of Cinder and her plight. I'd watched her shatter into a million pieces, had witnessed Crow giving a piece of himself to make her whole again, and despite all that, despite knowing she'll never break again, seeing something like that has to stay with you. Crow is handling it all far better than I would, and I suspect it's simply because he knows his woman is strong. Cinder isn't completely human, not like my Briella.

"They're protected right now," Briella points out. "They're all surrounded by the most powerful people we could find, but we do need to warn them."

Crow stands and looks off into the jungle in the direction of Gillikin and where his own heart resides. He's grown more powerful—we all are—but something about the longing I can feel rolling off him in waves has me moving closer to Briella so I can hold her hand. We've been blessed with mates amongst this time of turmoil. It's hard to leave them behind.

"When King and Red come," Crow speaks, still not looking at me. "You'll take a portal with Briella and get back to Gillikin so you can start preparations. I'll accompany them back."

I pause, understanding what Crow is telling me but hesitant to accept. "You're sure?"

He nods. "You can only take one person. Take Briella to safety and I trust you two to take care of Cinder until I return. King and Red will be a target so I'll accompany them to help should any threats appear."

Briella sighs and looks out where the two had disappeared. "I'm such a sucker for a good love story." Both Crow and I look at her with raised brows. "What? A bitch can be both a softie and a badass."

Crow snorts at her words and there's no question of the respect in his eyes. "No wonder you and Cinder get along so well."

With a grin, Briella winks at the Scarecrow, a man she once looked at in fear. "Your girl's a warrior with a heart of gold. Of course, we get along."

Though I want to smile at her words, I find myself staring off into the trees, somber.

"Tin? You okay?" she asks, her hand snaking over my chest and stroking through the clothing she'd sewn with her own hand. My mate's gifts always amaze me, her ability to take fabric and make something beautiful. She's an artist, and despite her fragile mortality, I love her with everything in my being. My heart beats for her and for her alone.

"Just thinking," I say.

"Of what?"

"How war dresses up monsters as saviors," I muse and look down at her. Something hangs heavy in the air around us, prophesy coming to pass.

This will be a war among monsters, different and yet alike. We're all just trying to keep what we have, all just trying to survive. I have something to fight for, something more than my people. I have a future.

Now, I just have to be the villain I'm meant to be in order to keep it.

CHAPTER THIRTY-TWO

K ing gave me yet another shirt to wear, the cream-colored fabric soft against my skin. It reaches down to the tops of my knees, shortening my stature, but I don't mind. The clothing smells like him and so I'm enveloped in his essence as we step back into town. The others are waiting for us, their eyes taking in every detail from my wild hair to the bite marks on both of our bodies, to the fact I'm now wearing a different shirt. A blush immediately spreads along my cheeks, alerting them to what had transpired out in the jungle even if they had somehow not known. There's no way they could not know.

When Briella grins at me, I know exactly what she thinks happened, and she's certainly not wrong. She wiggles her eyebrows at me and I have to fight the urge not to laugh at her antics.

I glance up at King, at the man currently holding my hand and refusing to release me. I didn't peg him as an affectionate lover, but clearly, I was wrong. Every now and then, his thumb strokes the back of my hand, reminding me of his warmth as if I could somehow forget.

There's no way I can ever forget the Lion of Oz.

"We've come up with a plan," Briella announces brightly, her eyes twinkling at me. Despite needing to discuss other things, I know she's dying to ask what happened.

King tilts his head. "Let us hear it."

"We all need to get to Gillikin," Tin says, taking over when Briella gestures to him. "Crow is going to accompany you two there on foot. Meanwhile, I'll portal with Briella to the city and warn everyone. We'll begin preparations for whatever is coming so that by the time you three get there, we'll be ready for Ananke and Toto." Tin's eyes glow with light that shouldn't be possible. The name the woman goes by sounds foreign and strong. It's the first time I've heard it and it gives me chills. "The three of you will have to move quickly to reach us before the war begins. None of us know how long we have but luckily, you're in Winkie Country rather than Quadling. At least, you're close."

"Close is relative," Crow grunts. "We're one quadrant over, yes, but still far enough away, it could take days if we don't hurry. Luckily, between the three of us, I think we move fast enough to make it in less than a day."

"We must inform my people that we're leaving," King nods. "And then we'll be prepared to go. None of them are fast enough to reach Gillikin before Toto and the woman come, but they need to be prepared for two things."

"Those are?" I ask, looking up at him.

"If they're attacked first before we're attacked, or. . .if we fail and Oz falls."

"If we fail. . ." Briella trails off and shakes her head. "I refuse to believe that's possible. We're strong, especially with the others joining us. The prophesy brought everything we need to win. We just have to do so."

"So we make no mistake," King agrees. "I agree to the plan. Tin, you take Briella and go now to prepare. We'll be a day behind you."

Tin, without waiting for another invitation, pulls something out of his coat pocket and points it away from us. The air begins to swirl with color and lights until a large circle opens, showing a city street of what I assume is Gillikin. He pulls Briella to his side and looks back at us.

"Hurry back. We don't know what you'll encounter on your journey, and we don't know what we'll encounter in Gillikin. Being separated weakens us."

"We'll be there within as little time as possible," Crow answers. "Tell Cinder I'll be there soon."

"Kick anything's ass that gives you hell," Briella commands. Her eyes find mine and we share a smile before they both walk through the portal together and it collapses behind them.

"A portal," I murmur, looking up at King.

"No time for wonder," Crow reminds us. "Gather your people and then we need to leave right away."

King nods and moves over to the man I'd once nearly killed when I couldn't control my change. "Call a meeting. Quickly. The time has come, Lopper."

The frog man's eyes widen. "It's here?"

King nods in reply and the man, Lopper, turns and begins shouting to the town. "Gather round. Gather in the square. Gather immediately!"

We all wait as those inside their homes come out, and when a large crowd is gathered of those who live close enough to the castle to be gathered, King steps forward to address them. I watch the way he commands them, see the shift in the people when they realize he's not quite the same as he was before. The realization that King has emotion again makes many of them stand taller. How long have they dealt with a Lion who was aloof?

Lopper stands front and center, his kind eyes watching King carefully, seeing everything. When his eyes trail over to me, I bow my head just slightly, confirming the question in his eyes. The small smile he gives me makes something in my chest unfurl and I know without a doubt, I'll protect him against anything that comes. He probably doesn't need it, but the care I see in his eyes for my Lion makes my decision for me. I'm going to protect him.

"The time has come for war," King begins, standing in front of his people like the King he is. Though he still wears his crown, he holds his hands wide in a nonthreatening manner, talking to them as equals. "The locks that hold Toto inside his prison have been released despite our best efforts to stop them. You all know the heaviness that has been hanging in the air, and I'm here now to inform you it's time."

"Should we arm ourselves?" someone in the crowd asks.

"Yes," King nods, "but the battle will not take place here as far as we know. Our enemies are coming for us so we're taking the war to Gillikin. There's no time for our quadrant to march to war, not with so many, but you can protect Winkie Country in my stead. There's the chance they could swarm the rest of Oz before they come our way and you will all need to protect yourselves." He hesitates. "If for some reason, we fall—"

"You won't fall," Lopper interrupts. "We have faith in you." His eyes glance toward me again and I smile. Those same words had once been directed at me.

"There are more weapons within the armory," King responds as he bows his head toward them. "We must leave to fight, but you're all welcome to protect yourselves from within the castle. It's yours to use as a fortress." Reaching up to the crown on his head, King removes it and steps toward Lopper. Carefully, he sets the golden crown on Lopper's head. "While I'm gone, Lopper will be in charge."

The frog man blinks at the heavy crown on his head, moisture at the corner of his eyes. "King—"

"I spent a long time not treating you like the friend you are, Lopper," King says, his expression soft. I expect Ophir to come forward, but when King touches his shoulder carefully, I blink in surprise. "This is the beginning of me making up for all the years I stopped caring."

"It wasn't by choice," Lopper argues. "I know what you gave up for us." His eyes meet mine. "What it took for it to be returned."

"We need to go," Crow reminds us, wincing at having to interrupt. "We must make hast."

"He's right," King sighs, stepping back. "Protect yourselves before you protect homes. Homes can always be rebuilt."

"We remember Toto well," someone says.

"We remember the massacre," another adds.

Lopper nods. "You will protect all of Oz," he tells us. He gestures to those behind him. "We'll protect Winkie as best as we can."

King stands tall and addresses the entire crowd who gathered for his words, his voice carrying around the square. "Remember, courage isn't the absence of fear," he reminded his people. "It's standing strong in the face of it."

I look at him with his words, at the profoundness of what he speaks, and understand what King had truly given up for Oz so long ago. It wasn't just his empathy. The Lion hadn't given up a simple emotion. He'd given up friends and people, care and connection. But now he's here, reminding everyone of their strength. Without fear, I thread my hand through King's and know I can face anything.

No matter if I'm afraid, I'll meet fear head on.

After all, I'm the beast I was always meant to be. . .

CHAPTER THIRTY-THREE

WHITE

I should be listening as Tin talks, trying to figure out where my place in the plan is. War is upon us as it always is. There never seems to be a moment where we're able to simply exist in happiness. Perhaps, we're not meant to sit idle and enjoy the love we've come to find. Perhaps, we'll never stop fighting for the right to have such full hearts.

I should be listening to the plan, figuring out what I need to do in order to prepare for war, but instead, my eyes keep trailing over to my mate where she sits amongst the others, her eyes glazed over. She's not listening either, her mind lost somewhere else. Normally, I wouldn't worry. Jupiter is often lost in the clouds when she's trying to figure out a solution, but this feels different. Something is wrong with my mate and I don't know what.

The other day, I'd caught her standing at the edge of the Grimm Forest, just staring into the darkness as if something inside was speaking to her. When I'd asked her, she'd said she simply heard something that caught her attention, but knowing how dangerous the woods are, Jupiter shouldn't have been standing there alone. We had a rule about being in pairs. I didn't tell her I suspected she'd been moments away from stepping into the trees, didn't explain I could feel something was wrong. We're connected far deeper than simply being in a relationship. Still, I've been waiting for her to come to me, to tell me what's happening inside of her. She hasn't, and I'm starting to worry I'm losing her to something far worse than the madness the Sons have dealt with in the past.

Right now, Jupiter sits silent amid the bustle of conversation and preparations, an unusual trait in the scientist. Her vials sit empty on the table beside her as everyone talks. Normally she would be sampling everything she can find, tucking it away for later. I can't remember the last time I've seen her do so now, can't remember her being excited at some small flower she'd discovered or a bug she found.

At first, I'd assumed it was stress. A lot has been going on and I know she's been worried about her powers being finicky. We're saving the world yet again, this time on a large scale because it affects more than one. We're going to war again. We have people who are vulnerable, including Clara and Aniya. We still have no answers for what's happening.

Jupiter is closing down in front of me, and I don't know how to help her.

My eyes flicker between checking on her and trying to listen to Tin and Briella explain what's happening.

"Red is a werewolf," Briella gushes, explaining the woman who broke King's lock. "You should have seen how King buckled—"

"We can discuss the love story later," Tin reminds her. "First, we need to get everyone armor who doesn't have it."

"Oh yes! I'm prepared for that!" Briella admits, and it doesn't surprise me. The woman has a talent for making clothing. She's probably been working on armor since she got here.

We had all heard the lock break, had felt it. At first, we'd panicked, but now, we have a plan. Gillikin is preparing for war, all the inhabitants of Tin's realm donning their weapons and getting ready to protect the city. Our numbers aren't what we'd had for war against Alice, but at least there's more of us with power.

I glance at Jupiter again where she sits silently, as if she can't hear a word of what's happening around her.

Atlas sighs where he stands on the outside of the circle. "I'm sure getting tired of fighting for our lives. Maybe we should try bowling for once."

Everyone laughs, even those that don't know what bowling is, but I can't keep my eyes from Jupiter. My mate doesn't even register my gaze, as if she can't feel it despite our connection. I try not to let that fuel panic, but it's difficult.

Clara is watching her, too, though she's being more discrete about it. How many are worried for my mate? How many know that something is seriously wrong?

"Jupiter," I call, trying to get her attention. I can't remember the last time she's eaten, don't remember when I last made sure she's gotten a meal. Shame fills me. Have I been neglecting my mate? But no, I swear I gave her food only this morning. Had she eaten it?

Everyone goes quiet when she doesn't answer me, watching carefully.

"Jupiter," I try again. No answer, so I say, "Dreamwalker?"

Her eyes clear and she looks up at me. For a moment, she looks right through me, as if I'm not even there, before her beautiful eyes focus on me. Those blue eyes are ringed with fire for a split second before she blinks, and it's gone. I'm not even sure if I saw it or imagined it, but I relish that she's looking at me. She's still there inside. She's not lost to madness.

"Yes?" she asks, blinking away the daze she'd been in.

"Are you hungry?" I ask, offering to get her a plate.

She shakes her head. "I'm full."

But I can't remember the last time I've seen her eat. Every instinct tells me something is wrong, that my mate is struggling against something. The story of her sister comes to mind, and I suddenly panic that the madness has found its way inside, that it's my fault she's like this.

Despite her saying she's full, I stand and prepare a plate filled with Oz fruits Tin explained were safe to eat before taking it to her. I take a seat beside her and pass it into her hands. Jupiter smiles gently at me, but it doesn't reach her eyes. I can feel Clara's eyes on us, can feel everyone continue their conversations so it's not so obvious they're watching and worried.

It takes everything in me to push down the panic so she can't see. Without caring what everyone else sees, I move to kneel before her, touching her knees gently until she meets my eyes.

"You have to eat, Jupiter," I urge, a bit of my worry bleeding into my voice.

"I told you," she says. "I'm full."

I meet her eyes, take in the fear there she's trying desperately to hide.

"Of what?" I ask.

Jupiter doesn't answer, but the way her gaze meets mine, I know the answer isn't food. Something is seriously wrong with my Dreamwalker, and I don't know how to help her. I don't know what enemy to fight. Instead, I lay my head against her knee and relish when she reaches out to caress my ear.

Still, my stomach twists in knots.

This isn't right. This isn't how it's supposed to be.

With a start, I realize Jupiter isn't wearing her signature shirts. Instead, it's a plain black shirt, and my heart squeezes painfully. Where's my Jupiter? Where did her color go?

In the distance, another howl echoes through Oz.

CHAPTER THIRTY-FOUR

RED

King, Crow, and I set out for Gillikin within an hour of Tin and Briella leaving, all three of us wearing not much else besides the clothing on our backs. Someone in the town had been kind enough to give me pants and a loose shirt to wear so I'm no longer in just King's oversized shirts. At least I won't have to hike through the jungle mostly naked. Someone had even given me boots to wear despite me saying I didn't need them. It's been so long since I've worn shoes, it almost feels uncomfortable not to feel the earth between my toes.

I carry no weapons except for the knife I'd stabbed King with. The blood has been cleaned away, leaving it sparkling. My look is completed with a bright red cloak King had gifted me.

"Just in case it gets cold," he claimed.

I didn't have the heart to remind him I no longer get cold, not with Feral a part of me.

Neither King nor Crow carry any weapons. My understanding is that none of us truly need a weapon, them less so than me. King himself is a weapon. Though I don't know what Crow can do, with his appearance and title, I assume he's strong enough to hold his own in a fight. We don't know what we'll encounter on our way to Gillikin, but at least we're well armed.

For a long time, we're silent as we pick our way through King's poisonous jungle. Every so often, a fly trap plant will get brave and attempt to take a bite out of either Crow or me. Every time, whoever it tries to bite takes great pleasure in shredding the plant until it's incapable of biting again. I watch Crow literally crush one in his fist, uncaring of the sharp teeth, before he looks back at us with a raised brow.

"So," he begins, breaking the silence. "Are we going to talk about the secret you've been keeping, King?"

King tenses in front of me, but Crow only raises his brow higher at the reaction. Meanwhile, I keep my lips clamped shut. It's not my secret to tell, nor is this conversation my business.

"Denial until the end, huh?" When King still doesn't answer, Crow shakes his head. "I'm not stupid. I don't know if Tin has put it together or not, but it's clear to me."

"And what is it you think is so clear?" King asks, his voice thick with warning.

Crow stops in his path before us and turns to look at him. I'm standing behind King, witnessing the confrontation and knowing that Crow has figured out the secret I've been keeping for the Lion. Realizing it's probably my fault he realized it, I clench my fists, but I don't run. I promised I wouldn't.

"King is a real person, but not the only person inside your head." King doesn't answer him, but Crow doesn't need him to. "There's no need to confirm. I already know. I'm simply curious how you've kept it a secret for so long. Is it a byproduct of giving up your empathy? Like how my soul worked?"

King hesitates for a moment but when I press my hand against his back in comfort, he glances over his shoulder at me and sighs. "No."

"So it's always been so." Crow blinks. "Well, I'm not sure how you handle it honestly, but there was really no reason to keep it a secret. That's hardly the strangest thing in Oz."

I look between them curiously. "Aren't you two. . .friends?"

"We're Heirs," Crow replies. "To be Heirs means to have no friends."

"How lonely," I mumble, thinking about how that must feel. I no longer have friends, didn't have many before, but I can see myself already building a friendship with Briella. It's not hard to open yourself up to connections.

"Things are changing though," Crow says, his words almost solemn despite their message. "So maybe one day, we'll refer to each other as friends first."

King rolls his eyes, shrugging off the words as if they're too sappy for him. Despite the look, I can see satisfaction in his gaze, as if he likes the concept of having friends again.

"Why do they let you be in charge all the time if you're such an asshole?" I ask, chuckling at King reaction. It blows my mind that Ophir and Fang sit back more often than not, leaving king to control everything even when he was without empathy.

The scathing look I get from King almost distracts me from the sound of a twig breaking from my left. Almost. I turn my head the same time as King does, both of us staring into the jungle at the sudden sound.

That's how we both miss the attack that comes from the right. Something explodes from the opposite direction, a flash that slams a burst of magic against the three of us. I'm blown backward, away from King and Crow, flying into the jungle as my body absorbs the impact.

The giggles fuel my fury as I slam into a tree and drop back to my feet with a snarl.

"Big mistake," I fume.

"That's what you think," a female voice giggles. "Silly little human. Follow the breadcrumbs and maybe we'll let you catch us."

I don't shift, keeping my secret, but I can't help my smile. I don't need breadcrumbs to hunt.

CHAPTER THIRTY-FIVE

A sinister laugh echoes around me as I move in the direction of the two enemies. Though I know I hold a secret in my arsenal, I'm still angry. How dare they attack people I care about? I'm going to rip the two to shreds happily, but first, I'll play the game. I stay in my human form, keeping up with the two creatures I chase. I don't know who they are or where they've come from—though I suspect—but Briella told me to destroy anything that attacks. I'm not going to let her down.

"Red!" King shouts, searching for me, and in response, I give a very human, generic howl to let him know my location. He can scent me, will likely be following based on that alone, but still, I help. It also lets him know that I'm still very much wearing my flesh and that I'm being led purposely away from them. They think to set a trap, but there's no caging me.

It's easy to track the two through the jungle, easy to follow their path. Either they're both terrible at hiding their tracks or they're purposely leading me in this direction. I'm certain they meant to separate us and have picked me out as the weakest link among the three of us. I'm King's weakness in their eyes. If they kill me, they'll double back and kill the others if they can, but not only will I not allow that, it would be impossible. They don't understand what I am, can't see that

I'm more than the human flesh I wear, but they've certainly underestimated Crow and King. They're Heirs for a reason.

"Chase, chase, chase," the female shouts with glee. "Come along, pretty girl!"

I slam through the trees, doing exactly as they ask, knowing they're setting a trap they think will get me. We're both playing a game. What they don't realize is I'm not the mouse here.

"You going to kill us with that little knife?" the male goads, running ahead of me, matching my pace so I don't gain or fall behind. I'm not running as fast as I can. I'm barely running at half my speed, but this is a speed a human would run at. A wolf hides her claws until she's ready to use them.

Feral is awake inside me and shifts restlessly in my chest, begging to be let out, desperate to retaliate.

"Not yet," I whisper to her. "Not yet." But soon. Very soon.

I slam through the tree line and onto the bank of the river I suspect comes from the same source as the waterfall I'd once thrown myself over. The two creatures I've been chasing stand on the bank, both grinning at me with glee. They'd be beautiful if not for the clear self-mutilation across their faces. Old cuts and scars form patterns I can't make sense of. Strange bumps and shape make them look more demonic than they should. Metal accents all the strange marking by cutting through their faces and adding to the sinister air. But if not for all the work to look sinister, they would have appeared as nothing more than human, only the magic swirling around them giving them away.

Both of them are dressed in leather clothing. The female's waist is cinched in by a corset but the male wears a loose shirt that reveals more mutilated skin down the gaping center. It's there I see the bite scars surrounded by tattoos of. . .candy?

"Look, Hansel," the female says. "Another human. The Heirs have a thing for them."

"Weak little things, Gretel," he agrees. "I don't see the appeal."

The corner of my lip quirks up at their assumptions. They're strong, but apparently, I gave them too much credit with it came to cleverness.

"So you must be the two causing trouble. You attacked the castle before." I recognize their scents, understand they were the ones that triggered my reaction before, but I'm not that Red anymore. I'm both Red and Feral. We are one.

"Clever human, even if she's weak," Hansel comments, bumping his shoulder with his sister. "What else do you know, weakling?"

"I heard of you two," I murmur, taking a slow step to the left, drawing their eyes. They move with me, thinking I'm cutting myself off by putting my back to the river. They think me stupid. "Back home in the Grimm Forest."

"Oh, a human from Grimm!" Gretel says gleefully. "Even better. What town did you come from?"

"It doesn't exist anymore," I reassure them. "I doubt you would know it. It was so small."

"And what did you hear about us?" Hansel asks curiously. Their egos beg for answers even as they think they corral me. It's so easy to keep them talking.

"That you cause chaos wherever you go," I murmur, stroking a hand mentally down Feral's spine to calm her. She paces in agitation inside me, waiting for the moment I call her forward. "That your father led you into the forest and left you to die. That a witch found you and tried to fatten you up. I remember the story of how you killed her and everyone in the surrounding towns after you glutted yourself on her power. If I remember correctly, you now have a taste for anything sweet after the witch forced you to eat."

"So, you *have* heard of us," Gretel murmurs, narrowing her eyes. "Did you also know we're World Breakers?"

I shrug. "That makes sense. Of course you'd like to cause trouble after your own father abandoned you."

"He was a coward," Gretel spits.

"You're right," I agree. "Any man who takes children into the forest and leaves them to die deserves a fate worse than death."

Hansel grins. "Which is exactly what he got." He grins at Gretel. "Think ole dad is still screaming, sister?"

"If his vocal cords still work," she replies gleefully. Her eyes meet mine. "You'll be screaming, too, little human. Just because you know who we are doesn't mean we'll spare you. We have our orders."

"World Breakers taking orders," I murmur. "How. . .quaint."

"Ananke a stronger World Breaker," Hansel purrs. "All the worlds will shatter beneath our feet."

"Sure," I agree. "As if she'll spare you when the deed is done."

Gretel's brows crinkle. "I grow tired of talking, Hansel."

The male grins and pulls out a knife "We're going to kill everyone you've ever loved," he promises me. "After we kill you and string you up as a gift for the Lion, we'll gut him and use his entrails to decorate your body like a piece of art. The only witnesses to your existence will be the maggots that feast on your body as you rot."

"How graphic," I say, tilting my head. "Please, go on."

Hansel blinks, as if he expected his imagery to scare me and he's at a loss for what to say next. Gretel, sensing his confusion, takes a turn.

"The Tin Man's mate, Briella. She's just as human as you are. How much fun we're going to have using her, brutalizing her body while forcing Tin to watch. Do you think he'll cry?"

Hansel laughs and lunges at me, clearly not intending to attack, but I jerk purposely, making him think he scared me. He laughs with glee, eager to cause pain, to inflict as much trauma as possible before he kills me.

Silly Hansel and Gretel, never quite learning who the real monsters are.

The part of the story I hadn't mentioned, of how their father hadn't been their father at all, but something else, some creature that had taken their father's place after killing both parents. They'd lived with the monster right under their noses until it had taken them into the woods and left them, tiring of taking care of the two children. I don't know who the monster was, don't know if they actually captured it like they said, but it only proves one thing.

Hansel and Gretel wouldn't know a monster if they were looking at one.

Clearly.

They don't know what I am. They only see a human.

"Red!" King shouts in the distance, too far away to help but growing closer.

Hansel laughs as if it's funny before mocking King's shout. "Red! Red! Red's dead! Red! Red!"

Gretel pulls out a knife and points it at me, a grin splitting chapped lips. "Run," she sneers. "For we like hunting little rabbits."

I bare my teeth at her when I grin, and she shifts uncomfortably, though she doesn't understand why. I don't need anyone's help, don't need King or Crow to come save me. I'm no damsel in distress. I'm the monster children fear.

"Good," I purr. "For I am no rabbit." I stroke my hand down Feral and give her control, letting her take over. My bones begin to pop, and Gretel takes a step back, her eyes wide in sudden horror. She knows what I am, understands what they've done. "I'm a wolf," I growl as I shift completely. Something shifts in my chest, something new, but I don't pay it any mind. I have another problem to address first.

With a snarl, I show them exactly the kind of monster I am and lunge.

CHAPTER THIRTY-SIX

KING

The screams echo around my jungle, and I panic. I don't know if Red's scream is in there, don't know if I can hear properly through my panic. I'm already cursing myself for allowing us to be taken by surprise. Before I even realized that Red was being separated from us, she was already sprinting through the trees, far enough away that it took me too long to chase after her. Hansel and Gretel had purposely spread their magic around Crow and me, disorienting us for long moments, and now I'm too far away from Red to help her.

"*Find her,*" Fang growls. "*Find her now.*"

"*King, we have to move faster,*" Ophir says, his voice filled with the same panic as mine.

"If something happens to her when I've just found her—"

"Just hurry," Crow interrupts, running alongside me. "We can stop the bastards."

Another scream, one filled with pure terror echoes around me, but it's not Red. That voice belongs to a male. Confusion fills me, and I don't know what we expect to find, but when we break through the trees and see the river, it's not what we find.

Both Crow and I slide to a stop at the sight before us, our eyes wide. At first, I think I'm seeing things, because nothing makes sense, not right away. Then I blink and everything comes into focus.

Red stands in the middle of the small clearing in her wolf form. She's completely Feral in this moment, but when her eyes meet mine, I see Red shining there. She's accepted who she is, has embraced herself, and I can see that knowledge shining in her eyes. Around her, swirling in the air, it looks like purple lightning bugs shifting in the air. I've only ever seen that sort of magic one other time, long ago. As we stare at her in shock, Red drops Hansel's shredded body from her claws and it hits the ground with a wet squelch. My eyes trace around the clearing and find Gretel's body where it lays ripped in pieces, scattered around the once green grass. Now it's stained crimson by the brother and sister's blood.

Crow stumbles back the same time as he captures the two souls shrieking in the clearing in his hands, holding them hostage even as he puts distance between himself and Red. There's true fear in his eyes, the second time I've ever seen it there. The first time was when he thought he lost Cinder. I don't blame him for his fear now, but this is Red. This is my wolf.

I take a hesitant step forward, the magic in the air sizzling my skin and leaving places raw. I ignore the bites of pain in order to move just a little closer.

"Red," I whisper.

Her eyes flash. "Feral," she growls. Blood drips from her muzzle and her claws, splatters across her fur. She'd saved herself, hadn't needed me, but something happened that none of us expected. My eyes glance between her and the fireflies again before focusing back on her eyes.

"One and the same," I clarify, watching her closely.

She tilts her head and I see Red there, see her knowledge at what's happened. "Before you can kill the monster, you have to say its name," she murmurs, understanding what she is. She lifts the knife she'd been carrying before and holds it out for me. It's perfectly clean except for where her fingers touch it. She hadn't lifted the knife to Hansel and Gretel even once. She hadn't needed to.

I shake my head, refusing to take the knife. "I don't need that."

"Do you know what I am?" she asks sadly. When I nod silently, she drops the knife to the ground. "Am I more of a monster than you imagined?"

I step closer, and though the magic burns, I ignore it in favor of holding Red's gaze. I just want to move closer to my wolf, to my Red. "We're all monsters," I say. "Remember?"

Without saying another word, her bones begin to pop. Fur begins to shed, leaving behind perfect pink skin that adjusts to her new shape as she shrinks and groans at the change. There's not as much pain anymore as she shifts, not a struggle, and it's confirmation of what I already know.

Red and Feral have merged fully.

Her bones continue to pop until she stands before me in shredded clothing that barely conceals her. I quickly tug off my own shirt and hand it to her, an action that's becoming all too common. I should start preparing ahead and packing her extra clothing.

When she pulls it on and looks up at me with bright, understanding eyes, a soft smile tugs at her lips. "It just matters what kind of monster you choose to be," she says, repeating my words from before back to me. It seems my wolf has finally decided what she is. The magic around her dissipates, releasing the buzzing along my skin with it, but it's not gone. It lives inside of her now.

I glance back at Crow where he still stands staring at Red with wide eyes. The souls are still in his fists, struggling without sound as if he silenced them.

"King. . ." he says, but no other words follow.

"She's on our side, Crow," I remind him, prepared to protect her if necessary.

"But she's a—"

"Lobo," I finish, looking back at my female, at the way she watches the exchange. Her eyes meet mine and something passes between us. We're far better matched than even I thought. "I know." She tilts her head at me, and I smile. "All that blood looks good on you," Fang purrs through me. "It really brings out your eyes."

"Oh, for fuck's sake," Crow growls behind us. "We need to get to Gillikin before you two start fucking here in front of me."

"What?" I ask, still staring at Red in wonder.

"Something far larger is happening than you're thinking about right now," Crow growls, drawing my attention.

"And what's that?" Red asks, her voice soft as she looks over at Crow where he's clearly agitated.

He steps forward and I tense in case he attacks, but instead of threatening Red, he looks her in the eyes. Without flinching, he lifts first one soul to his mouth and swallows it whole, the new trick he'd picked up. He does the same for the second, ensuring they're never released in the world again. "Not only are you a lobo, but you just killed not one, but *two* World Breakers with your bare hands." He scowls. "They were weaker ones, but still."

Red frowns in confusion but I jerk, realizing what Crow is saying. We've only just learned about it from the Wonderlanders, only just understand what might happen in this war. It isn't supposed to happen like this. "Fuck," I grunt.

The worlds begin to shudder beneath our feet.

CHAPTER THIRTY-SEVEN

RED

"When a World Breaker dies, things become unbalanced and they need to be balanced again," Crow says, his eyes on the bodies of Hansel and Gretel behind me. "That's what has been thought by the others. Thus, the worlds will shake with the new transfer."

"And how do you know this?" I ask, watching him carefully. It's clear he still hasn't relaxed completely around me, and I don't blame him. If the last interaction they had with a lobo was with Toto, then clearly, I will unnerve him. I hadn't realized what I am, would have never guessed that I can wield magic. And yet here I am, doing just that.

I can feel the power in my veins, a sizzle that neither burns nor hurts me, but it's ever present. They feel like stars, so bright, it's almost difficult to look inside myself at them. I've never felt so. . .vibrant, but once the magic appeared, I knew it had always been there, dormant. Not only had accepting Feral been a factor, but within the same moment, I had killed Hansel and Gretel. It had been the perfect mixture of events to awaken the magic. Now, I feel strong, stronger than I've ever felt. I feel invincible, though I'm sure that's not the case.

"Wonderland went to war with a World Breaker," Crow answers my earlier question. "They killed her. To balance it out, they all became more powerful. Clara became the Empress at the behest of whatever powers control things." His eyes trace over me, but there's nothing sexual about it. He's evaluating me. "I'm assuming your magic awakening is the balance for one death, but there must be balance somewhere else. And I don't feel any different since the last time I gained a power." Crow looks over at King. "Do you?"

"No," King shakes his head. "I still feel the same as before Hansel and Gretel died."

My chest squeezes. "So someone else is likely changing right now?"

Crow nods. "I assume so. Somewhere, someone here in Oz will be changing. It'll be someone who was likely already hanging in the balance. It's just a matter of who. So many of us have felt our powers fluctuate lately. So many powerful people together seems to be having an effect on things, but I can't point to one specific person without being in Gillikin to witness it."

"So someone else is in danger right now and we don't even know who," I breathe.

If not for King storming into the clearing after I'd killed the two World Breakers, there's no telling what I would have done. Could I have run off into the forest and started my own rampage of death? Could I have hurt someone? Both had been possibilities if I was so lost in bloodlust, I didn't realize what I was doing. But I'd also been working to merge with Feral for so long now, perhaps, it would have never happened. Whoever else may be affected by my killing will have no warning. They won't know what's happening, won't understand.

"We need to get to Gillikin right now," King grunts. "And we need to move fast."

Crow looks to me. "Can you keep up?"

I know he's not trying to insult me. King and Crow are Heirs. They were both more powerful than me before I'd killed Hansel and Gretel. It's not out of the question that he would still think so. How can he know what I've become? How can he understand the increase in power?

"I can keep up in wolf form," I inform him before tugging off the shirt King had given me. It's stained with blood where it had touched my skin, but he pulls it on without question, uncaring. The moment I'm free of the clothing, I invite Feral forward. The shift happens far faster than it used to. There's less pain as my bones pop and rearrange. My insides no longer feel like someone stirs them. Instead, the shift is fluid as I stand taller than my human form and roll my shoulders, a few of the purple stars dancing from them to light the air.

King's face lights up as he watches me shift, realizing exactly how far I've come since the first time I slammed into his quadrant, determined to fight him. With one more second to spare, his hand brushes down my side in a caress, letting me know exactly how he feels about my progress.

With a toothy grin, I wink at him. I'm sure it's a strange sight when I'm in my wolf form, but his smile only widens.

"Good," Crow says. "Time to run."

We need to get to Gillikin far faster than we originally planned for. There are too many threats now, too many problems.

Without waiting for another order, the three of us push ourselves into a sprint, running through Winkie Country at speeds that would be impossible if we were human. Of course, none of us are so simple as to be only human. The jungle trees speed by, none of the poisonous plants reaching out to touch us as we fly by. The jungle I'm used to slowly changes from damp trees to creepy ones as we pass into Gillikin. The neon city beckons us as we draw closer and it's with that, I realize how much I've truly changed.

We just made a few hours trip in fifteen minutes.

More stars bleed from my shoulders, but they follow.

They'll always follow now. . .

CHAPTER THIRTY-EIGHT

ANANKE

The worlds begin to rumble beneath my feet, and I feel the shift between them. It shouldn't have been odd at this point, not with how much chaos this new world I find myself in contains. Something about this shift, however, feels different.

I feel it a few seconds after the ground begins to shake and I whirl, my eyes studying the world around me as if that'll add to the clarification, but I already know what's happened. I can feel the deaths.

"Weaklings," I hiss. "They got themselves killed."

Rumple is standing silently against the wall. I can't remember the last time he spoke to me, can't remember the last time he did anything other than follow my orders. Useless. As useless as the siblings when they went and got themselves killed. Fools!

Toto stands beside me, his own nose in the air, scenting the power shift. "Something else is happening," he growls, scenting something I can't.

I don't know what he senses that I don't—I don't really care—but I know we no longer have time. The more time we give them, the more power they'll amass. If I want to destroy every world, I have to start with them. They're my only obstacle.

I reach up and caress Toto's jaw. He leans into the touch, starved for the attention after being locked up so long. There's no romance in the gesture on either of our parts, only a transaction of sorts. There will never be any romance for me again.

"It matters not, darling," I remind him. "I think it's time we make our move. What about you?"

Toto grins with his canine teeth, a strange expression on one so beastly. "Yes," he purrs. "My minions are ready."

"Then let us progress."

I turn toward Rumple, but the trickster is no longer there. The place he stood is empty and there's no sign he was ever there to begin with. Clever of him, even if it makes me scowl at his absence.

"Coward," I hiss under my breath, leaving him to his own fate. Now isn't the time to give chase. The worlds will end regardless and he's a part of at least one of them.

As Toto goes to gather the flying monkeys he controls, I press my hand to my stomach and tilt my head up into the air. "They'll all pay, *der Säugling*. Don't you worry. They'll pay."

I swear I hear a baby cry in answer, but I don't turn toward it. It's only more phantoms, and I can'd afford any more phantoms until I destroy the world around me.

Only then will I follow the phantom into oblivion.

CHAPTER THIRTY-NINE

JUPITER

My stomach knots in tangles as I stand in the middle of the street with the others, my eyes going between seeing all and glazing over. My mind has been lost in the clouds lately, making it difficult to keep focused on any one topic. I haven't been able to think passed the swirling feeling in my chest, my whole body revolting against the sensation. My stomach revolts against the sensitivity there and I know I'm going to be sick if I move too much. I press my hand over it in worry, turning to see if there's somewhere I can move to collect myself, but White finds me before I can escape.

"What's wrong?" he asks, clear concern in his eyes. He's been so worried about me lately and I'm a terrible liar. I can't keep telling him I'm okay when I'm not, but I don't have any answers to give him. I don't know what I'm feeling, if I'm okay, but something is. . .off. Besides my powers acting strange and erratically, my mind is wandering more and more lately. Am I sick? Does sickness reach into Oz?

"I'm fine," I say, not meeting his eyes. I've never been one to avoid his gaze, never been one to shy away.

"Jupiter," he chastises, reaching forward to cup my chin. Carefully, he draws my gaze back to his and I almost flinch away from the emotions swirling in his eyes. "I can't help you if I don't know what's going on."

The tips of my fingers begin to tingle the same moment as the ground beneath our feet begins to rumble. We can't afford the chaos that comes with another world moving into our path, but we can't do anything to stop it. Another problem I haven't figured out how to stop. Another problem added to the ever-growing pile.

"I don't know what's going on," I finally admit, pressing my hand harder into my stomach. I'm going to be sick. I know I am. Whatever this feeling is, I can't contain it. I haven't eaten in days, but I suddenly feel as if my stomach is full, like I've just eaten far too much.

White is studying me, his brows furrowed in concern. I know what he sees. White isn't stupid. He understands that there's something wrong, but he doesn't know how to help. He doesn't even reach out to take my hand for fear that it'll be too much. Because I love him with everything in my soul, despite the needles suddenly stabbing into my skin all over, I take his hand with my own shaking one and squeeze in comfort.

"White," I whisper, and my voice comes out just as shaky as my body. "I'm scared."

His face softens and something inside him cracks at the fear in my voice. "Tell me how I can help," he pleads. "I don't know how to help."

"Knowing you love me helps," I tell him, and it's true. Though I'm in pain, though my body feels like it's about to explode, knowing he's here for me stills something in my mind. I'm not alone in this. I won't ever be alone. But I have to tell him something, to bridge the gap and admit what I do know. "There's something stirring inside me," I murmur, and my voice cracks on a sob catching in my throat. "I don't know how to control it, how to wield it. I'm sick with it."

White moves closer and wraps his arms gently around me. His hold sends violent bursts of pain beneath my skin, but I don't say a world. I want to be helped, to be reminded that maybe it'll all be okay, even if it doesn't feel like it will be. I want to be loved. I love my rabbit. I love my rabbit. *I love my rabbit.*

"Let me help," he murmurs into my hair where it hangs around my shoulders. "Let me help you."

Another sob comes up my throat and catches there. When I open my mouth, it escapes before I can get the words out and White hugs me tighter, more painfully. My skin. *Oh god, my skin!* "I'm terrified I'm turning into a monster," I cry, hugging him just as tightly despite the pain. Something inside me tells me not to waste this moment, not to give it up no matter the forces trying to make me.

"You could never be a monster," White protests. "You'll always be my Jupiter, Dreamwalker, scientist, mate. There's nothing monstrous in you."

I want to say more, to argue, but everything inside of me suddenly comes to a complete standstill. The pain pauses. The feeling in my stomach holds on the edge of the cliff, as if I'm on the verge of puking. My hair stands on end around me, as if the air is electrified. My first thought is that I'm having a seizure. Insanely, in the middle of these strange feelings, I can suddenly think clearly enough to attempt a diagnosis, but the moment it crosses my mind, I dismiss it. This is Oz. I'm not in my world. There's something far more wrong happening to me than a seizure.

"White," I whisper, but my voice is suddenly strange even to my own ears. Apparently, White thinks the same thing. He pulls back just enough to look in my eyes and his own widen in shock.

"Jupiter, your eyes. . ."

My heart struggles inside my chest. I can't feel my legs, can't feel the tips of my fingers. My breath stops in my lungs and squeezes tightly. What's wrong with my eyes?

And then the very air around me freezes in anticipation.

Something shifts inside me, changes me, keeps me in stasis for what feels like forever but in reality, is only a few seconds, and then that change explodes.

Power slams inside of me with a violence that has my back bowing. That same power throws White away from me, and his fingers are ripped from mine. I shriek, the sound ear-piercing as something arrows inside my chest, and again, and again. My skin is peeled from my body and replaced before the act is repeated. With certainty, I know I'm

157

going to die. Someone can't handle this much pain and come out on the other side.

My spine snaps.

Somewhere in the distance, I hear White screaming. There's terror in that sound, desperation, as he shouts for the others. There's no help. Not anymore. I can't be saved.

I feel my vocal cords tear as I continue to shriek, damaging them, and I can't breathe. I still can't breathe. My heart bursts inside my chest and reforms, building back piece by piece until it feels stronger. Then it repeats the process again, and again, and again.

And then, just as suddenly as the power rips me to shreds, it stops.

I'm shaking as I straighten, as I look through eyes I know are ringed with fire. That purple fire oozes through my brains, takes over, and there's nothing inside me. I'm everything. I'm nothing. I am the stars and the cosmos wrapped in flesh.

The man before me hesitantly steps forward, his hand held out like I'm a frightening animal. The corner of my lips curl up in amusement. Me, the frightened animal? Compared to a rabbit?

"Jupiter?" White says. His hand is shaking as he extends it toward me, but I understand he's not afraid of me. He should be. I am the burning stars. But instead, he's afraid for me.

When he gets close enough, I reach up with a steady hand and cup his cheek. He immediately presses into my touch despite the sizzles that zap along his skin at my new power.

"Are you. . .okay?" he asks, his silver eyes meeting mine despite the power in my veins. He's not afraid of my power. But I'm no longer just Jupiter. I'm no longer just. . .me, and I don't know how to control that.

The power unfurls in my chest at our touch, reaches toward my mate. . .my mate. . .my. . .mate.

The voice that slips from my lips is almost not mine. It is many and yet not. It is too much.

"Poor little white rabbit, so lost in time," I murmur, the fire spreading along my fingertips. "You'll lose track of everything in this world, including your mind."

158

White's eyes widen just before my power snaps toward him, desperate to take everything he is, determined to take what he offers.

My mate. My mate. My mate.

White screams as the power spears inside him, takes him, wants him.

My mate. . .

CHAPTER FORTY

RED

The emerald green castle in the distance stands like a beacon of war. Above it, dark clouds begin to swirl just as strange flying creatures begin to swarm from inside the castle, spinning around the clouds as if caught in some sort of vortex. I've never seen anything like it, have never seen a castle so bright. From all directions, those creatures add to the swarm, building it, amassing an army of them. We have to keep moving, fast, faster, faster!

I don't understand what's happening, but King and Crow seem to. Their eyes watch the creatures with disgust and annoyance.

"What are they?" I breathe, focusing between looking at the growing cloud and the trees in front of me. The neon city grows closer, beckoning us forward as we run.

"Flying monkeys," King growls.

"Horrible creatures with only blood on their minds," Crow adds. "Somehow, Toto always seems to sway them into following his lead."

"We once tried to wipe them out," King continues, keeping up beside me despite his human legs.

"And?"

"We failed," King answered with a raised brow. "Clearly."

Great, I think. Creatures that are so many, we'll be fighting them until we're either all dead or Toto is.

We move so fast, the trees blur by even as Gillikin comes into focus before us. Something inside me says we need to move faster, that things are happening and we need to be there for them. I need to be there for them. I don't know if I could have kept up with Crow and King in my human form, but the more I settle into the power in my veins, the more I think I could have. Still, there's nothing to be done about it right now. I'm already Feral, already more than keeping up. We're almost there. Once we make it, I can shift back.

We pass inside the border of the actual city within the Tin Man's domain, but Crow and King are sliding to a stop before I can follow them, making me rush forward a few more steps before I catch myself. Familiarity hits me, as if I've been here before, as if I've met someone here, an older man that whispered in my mind. When had I been here? When I was trapped as Feral?

Before us, there's a group of people rushing around a large golden orb of power, frantically trying to find a way in. The gold calls to me, asks me to join it, but I hold myself back, confused. Why on earth would it be calling to me?

"What is happening?" King asks, staring at the same thing I am. "What is that thing?"

Crow frowns. "Could it be the power—"

"Yes," I interrupt. "That's what it is."

Both men look at me in confusion. "How. . ." King trails off, his eyes taking me in.

"It feels familiar, like a sibling." I meet his eyes. "And I'm an only child."

A woman comes running up to us, her blue eyes as wide as her hair is wild. She's frantic as she throws herself at Crow and wraps her arms around him. When his own arms curl around her, I know this must be his mate, Cinder. She's beautiful, especially in the neon lights around us, as if she's some sort of violent angel. When she moves in the light, I almost think I see cracks in her skin, but when she releases him and lets go, they're not there anymore. A trick of the light or real?

Briella comes running up a second later, her hair loose from her braid. She's wearing something that looks more like armor now than a suit, but still made with skilled fingers. "We have a problem," she says by way of greeting. An older man is behind her, one that's somehow in my memories. Feral whines in excitement and it takes everything in me not to let the sound escape my lips. "Well, multiple problems."

Cinder looks up at me standing in my wolf form, her eyes wide. "Uh, are you another problem?"

"No," I answer as sparks of power bleed from my shoulders. I tuck Feral away and shift back to my human form, taking the shirt King offers me and tugging it on. Her eyes widen impossibly further.

"What a badass!" Briella says, her facing lighting up as I return fully to my normal form. I'd forgotten she hasn't seen me completely in my wolf form before, only in between shifts before I'd controlled them. "I knew I liked you, Red! I'll get you something better to wear as soon as we address some of the problems."

"What problems?" Crow asks, his eyes alight with magic I can only describe as feeling like death. Whatever power balances have changed in the world, I can feel the newness of Crow's magic, as if it's different than it once was, but I don't know Crow. It should be impossible to know that.

"First problem," Cinder answers. "Toto is released and as you can see, they're gathering for war. We're still gathering everyone. Gillikin is preparing for battle, but we've called anyone who can help against the flying monkeys. Those of us with enough power, we're going to be facing the World Breakers."

A young woman stands in the middle of the street behind them, drawing my eyes. Creatures surround her, sitting and standing with her, as if in protection as she looks up at the growing storm of flying monkeys. Something about her calls to me, something about her power, and I know without a doubt, despite all the new power in my veins, this girl is far more powerful than I am. Still, our powers are somehow linked, as if they're kin.

"And what other problems are there?" King asks, his eyes on the golden orb.

Briella winces. "Jupiter."

162

I look away from the young woman and furrow my brows when I focus on Briella. "Jupiter?"

"The White Rabbit's mate," Crow answers, his eyes searching the crowd. "I don't see either one of them.

"Are they okay?" I ask, my stomach clenching because I already know.

Briella's wince grows wider. "Ummm. . .not exactly."

CHAPTER FORTY-ONE

I stand on the edge of the golden orb with King and Crow beside me. Everyone is frantically moving around it, searching for a weakness and a way in, but I can't see one. I can't even feel a weakness, and that alone scares me. I'm tempted to reach out my hand and touch the orb, but something holds me back. Fear at what I'll be able to do stills my movement. Do I want to know what I really am?

The White Rabbit and his mate are locked inside, her powers too intense to control. No one knows anything other than the two were talking and then Jupiter starts to scream. When she stopped and touched White, the orb exploded out of her and locked them inside. We can't see them, the walls opaque, so I assume they can't see us.

"I guess we know who the power chose," I murmur to King, biting my lip.

"She's dangerous." Fang's voice.

I look over at him. "So am I," I remind him.

"Yes, but you're mine."

"And Jupiter is an integral part of this group." I glance back at the large congregation of flying monkeys still swirling above the castle. "And we could use all the help we can get right now."

A woman steps forward, her stomach heavily round with child. My eyes fall down to the weakness and widen, taking her in. She's so large, she must be due any day. "We can't get inside. Hatter won't even let me try."

"You're vulnerable," a man in a top hat—Hatter, I assume—growls. "You're not endangering yourself or the baby. We need another solution."

"Someone has to be strong enough to get inside," a man I've already been told is Cheshire argues. "None of us are, but that doesn't mean someone isn't." His eyes go to the young woman I'd watched earlier, as if singling her out, but no one says a word. She's just a child. I wouldn't want to send her either no matter how powerful she is.

There'd been quick introductions, but I think I have everyone's names correct as they switch between arguing and desperately trying to find a solution. No one seems to be able to push though so I don't even try. I'm just a wolf from the Grimm Forest. Despite my mental dismissal, I can feel the lie. Something within me says I should try, but that same fear has me curling my fingers with King's instead.

As they argue, my eyes trail over to the trees cutting strangely through Gillikin City, the trees calling to me. Once, I'd called part of them home, but now, they only feel like they belong to someone else. It doesn't stop the call though. Some part of me, some deep part, still belongs there.

Atlas shifts into some sort of large blue creature and pushes against the golden orb but whatever it's made of doesn't like his power. It shoves him backward violently enough to slide along the yellow brick. Tink runs up to him but he's on his feet before she gets there. They both check his body over, making sure he's not injured before he shifts back.

"My Berserker magic doesn't work either," he growls in frustration. "What the hell are we going to do? We can't leave them in there."

Hook stands with his arms crossed, his expression solemn. "What do we do if she's no longer safe?"

Everyone pauses.

"That won't be a problem," Clara retorts, her eyes hard. "She'll be okay. We just need to get inside and help her."

"Hook is right," Wendy says softly. "Jupiter is my friend, but if she's no longer Jupiter, we have to prepare for—"

"Stop it!" Clara growls, and despite her condition, power snaps out with her words. It's suddenly easy to see how she could be an empress. "We do not leave people behind. We'll do everything we can to save her and only when there's no hope, we'll discuss other options."

I'm watching them argue, wondering what I can do to help, when the young woman appears beside me. Without a word at first, she threads her fingers through mine on the opposite side of King. I know her name now, know she's the daughter of Tiger Lily and Peter Pan. I understand her power despite everyone mentioning something else, but though our powers reach out and touch in recognition, there's no comparison. Mine is like a muted down version of what she carries, and that should scare me. Instead, her large, innocent eyes put me at ease.

King glances over at me and does a double take when he sees Aniya holding my hand. He shifts as if to get in between us but I shake my head, telling him I'm fine.

"Hello, Aniya," I tell her, staring into eyes full of stars. I don't shy away from her power as it washes over me. I'm not afraid of it.

"Only we can get inside, Scarlett," she answers.

I blink. "How do you know my real name?" I'd been introduced as Red to everyone. No one besides King and Briella know my real name and I doubt anyone had time to inform the girl.

But Aniya doesn't answer, not at first. She tightens her hold and takes a step toward the golden orb, forcing me a step closer.

"Wait—"

"You know it as well as I do, Scarlett," Aniya says. "No one but you and I can step foot inside the power bubble."

"You're not going inside," Tiger says suddenly, having heard the words. "It's too dangerous."

Aniya turns to look at her mother. "*Makua*, you know I have to help. Would you rather me leave her to hurt when I can help?"

Peter is frowning, staring at where our hands are linked. "But why Red?" he asks.

The March Hare shifts beside them, nervous but not wanting to interrupt. Clearly, he cares for Aniya just as much as they do, desperate to swoop her up and protect her, but there's also understanding in his eyes. Aniya is meant for remarkable things. They won't always be able to protect her from the evil in this world.

Aniya smiles at March, settling his nerves down just a little, before she glances back at her father. Then Aniya looks up at me, her eyes sparkling. "Because she has the stars, too."

Peter's eyes widen but he nods in understanding even if I don't really know what it means. Sure, I have magic in my veins now, but stars? They do feel like stars. I even called them that, but had it just been a comparison, or had I unknowingly described exactly what they are?

King steps around us at her words, his fingers still in mine. "You're not going in there," he growls at me. "Not without me."

"It won't let you in, Lion," Aniya says before I can answer. "But you're welcome to try."

Knowing Aniya is right because I can feel the truth in her words somehow, I squeeze his claws reassuringly. "I'll be in and out before you know it," I promise.

"It's too dangerous—"

"Would you have me leave this woman to die? Knowing that I can help her?" I release his hand to reach up and caress his jawline, sadness in my eyes. "I've taken so many lives because I couldn't control the monster I am. This is my chance to start making up for that. This is my redemption."

Understanding passes over his eyes and I know he won't stop me, not in this. If I'm to be a good monster, I have to start acting like it. "If something happens to you—"

"I'll be fine," I promise, though I know I can't really keep it if the world decides otherwise.

King nods and presses a quick kiss to my lips. "Hurry back, little wolf."

Releasing him to look down at Aniya, I take a deep breath and release it. "Okay, I'm ready."

Clara comes up to us and takes both of our hands. "Bring them out safe," she implores us. "Please."

Together, Aniya and I step up to the edge of the golden orb, the young woman in charge more than me.

"You're going to wanna shift for this," she warns, looking up at me.

I don't question it. Instead, I urge Feral forward and my bones snap until I'm standing tall as my wolf. Aniya knows more than anyone else. Whatever she says, I'm going to trust her.

Before we touch the orb, I look over my shoulder to where King stands. My purple fireflies dance around me, declaring what I am to everyone watching that might understand it. I can tell not everyone does, but now isn't the time to explain it.

"I'll be back before you know it," I tell King.

"You better be," he growls back, but it's not a warning. It's a plea.

Turning back to the orb, I squeeze Aniya's fingers gently, and as one, we both step forward.

CHAPTER FORTY-TWO

The power that bites at my skin is brutal and piercing, as if filled with tiny shards of glass that burrow inside my flesh. Still, I continue to step through with Aniya, worried that she feels the same thing as I do. The power is still familiar despite the pain, and I understand the power bites because it's not being controlled. Jupiter hasn't accepted it. She's fighting it, and just like I'd once been terrified of Feral, it's easy to feel Jupiter's terror is the same.

Though I struggle to walk through the power, Aniya seems to walk through it with ease at my side. She doesn't show any discomfort at all, as if this is the easiest thing in the world for her. Power makes all the difference.

"Why bring me if you could just walk through it alone?" I grunt, pushing hard to make my way through, but the orb gives and lets me pass with pressure.

Aniya looks up at me with bright eyes. "Because your magic recognizes her magic. They're connected."

"How do you know so much?" She's so young, barely thirteen if I guessed, and yet her soul is so old, it makes my bones ache.

"I just do," she shrugs with a smile. "We're almost to the center. Brace yourself."

She's not kidding. The closer we get to the center of the orb, the more painful the power bites at me, until it feels as if it will rip me to shreds if it wants to. Just when I think I might not make it, we break through the golden orb's walls and stand in the center where there's no movement. There's no sizzling energy, no bite of pain, no wind. It's as if time has completely stopped within.

"That's because it has," Aniya says out loud despite me never having spoken. I should fear her, but something inside me says she's not evil. She's just powerful, and just like me, she's chosen the sort of monster she wants to be.

We're the good monsters.

In the middle of the orb, a woman sits on the ground cross-legged. A man with rabbit ears has his head on her lap, his eyes closed, his body limp. Red hair falls around the woman's face to hang around her, hiding her face from our view at first. As we step inside, she looks up at us, her eyes haunted, tear tracks running down her cheeks. White hot fire rings her irises, and more of the sparks I've felt circle around her. Where mine are purple, her sparks are a mixture of green and yellow. Jupiter and White look pristine here, as if time has truly stopped for them. Such power. . .Hansel and Gretel didn't have these powers. I wonder at how the power changes to fit the person. I wonder where the powers change enough to fit the person but are still similar enough for our powers to recognize each other as kin.

"I broke him," Jupiter says, her voice hollow. Despite there being barely any emotion in the sound, I can feel her anguish. True, heart-breaking pain fills her at the thought of harming her mate, and I understand why she hasn't accepted her power. For the same reason, it took me too long to accept Feral.

"He's not broken," Aniya counters and releases my hand to move forward. She gently kneels down and places her hand on White's forehead. "He's locked."

A sob breaks through Jupiter's lips even though her face is mostly serene. Despite the power in control, she's still there. The emotions are so great, they break through despite the blanket of coldness. It's as if she's also locked, just like White is.

"How do we unlock him?" I ask.

"Jupiter must do it," Aniya answers and the woman flinches. Aniya reaches for me, and I move forward to take her hand, kneeling down beside them in my wolf form. "It will take you both recognizing the stars in your veins."

"The stars?" Jupiter parrots.

"The magic you feel," I clarify and gesture at the sparks around us. "You have to accept them to control them."

Jupiter's eyes crinkle in pain. "But what will I become?"

"Whatever you want to be," I say. "At all times, we have the possibility of being a good or bad monster. Which one you choose is up to you."

She blinks at me, at the words that had once helped me accept who I am. "I choose to be a good one."

I nod. "As I did." I offer her my hand. "So let's be good monsters together."

She hesitates for a moment, before she lifts a shaking hand to mine, and our palms meet.

"Find your stars, Dreamwalker," Aniya murmurs. "Therein lives your answer."

And then she steps away from us and takes up a spot against the edge of the golden orb, watching us carefully. It's strange to see her without her creatures, but I understand she left them outside for their protection. The little girl has a gift with monsters. It makes sense that she would understand us.

"I don't know what I'm doing," I offer as an apology when I meet Jupiter's fire-rimmed eyes.

Something sparks in those eyes, a piece of who she is beneath the power. "Then we'll guess together." She breathes. "After all, science is just a bunch of guesswork."

I don't know what her words mean but I trust her anyways when her voice echoes with power. Together, holding hands, with White between us, we close our eyes.

"Find the stars," I repeat on a whisper.

I feel the moment we both begin to glow brighter than even the neon city we find ourselves in. Like shooting stars in a long lost galaxy, our powers slam together with a violence that shakes the world.

CHAPTER FORTY-THREE

KING

"I can't see," I growl, pacing along the outside of the orb. "I can't see them. Can anyone see?" I ask, pacing faster, growing agitated. I'm not patient enough for this. I need to know what's happening. I need to see!

"Calm down," Tin grunts, watching the orb carefully. They all are. Despite the growing storm of enemies behind us, we're all silent, waiting for a miracle. "None of us can see."

"Easy for you to say when your woman is out here," I snap, running my claws along the orb. The power sizzles against them but doesn't throw me backward as violently as it had the Berserker.

Tin freezes. "Are you claiming her then?"

My face twists in annoyance. "Of course, I am, idiot. I broke the lock for her."

Briella's face lights up even as Tin's remains shocked. I watch as she claps her hands once before realizing that my mate is inside an orb that none of us understand. She meets my eyes.

"She'll be okay," she says, putting as much belief in the words as possible.

Everyone is silent for a moment, taking in what's happening, but it's Crow who breaks the silence to reveal something I should have revealed with Red here. It's her secret to tell, not ours.

"She's a lobo," Crow says into the silence.

I tense as everyone shifts in surprise. Tin and Azalea tense, both likely realizing it when the stars bled from Red's shoulders, but I'm quick to hold up my hand.

"She's not like Toto," I protest. "She's not evil."

"Definitely not," Briella agrees, and I'm so thankful for her, that I know I'll give her anything she needs for defending my female. "Red isn't dangerous to us. She's on our side."

Tink sighs from her place along the edge. Her appearance always confuses me because she always seems like she should have wings but the space on her back is completely empty. Someone called her a pixie once, but I can't imagine a pixie without wings.

"Prophesy," she breathes. "The world always provides what's needed when we need it. Toto is an evil lobo. Red is a good one. Balance. It's always about balance."

The Flamingo, a friend from long ago that I can recognize I haven't treated with the respect he deserves since he's arrived, looks out over Oz to the growing cloud of flying monkeys. There are so many collecting together now. The last time Flam was here, we'd attempted to wipe out the flying monkeys. We had stories of cutting through the mass of creatures together only to fail in the end. He looks uneasy now at the growing storm and I don't blame him. It had been a brutal war where we'd had to admit defeat, only because their numbers are too great. There's no extinction for the likes of those creatures.

"The flying monkeys are getting closer," he comments, his arms crossed. He still wears the pink leather I remember him in, but the woman at his side, though I don't know her, is as familiar as he is. Flam had never stopped speaking about his Dodo bird when he was here last and though he's beautiful and scary, there's a softness to her I only understand because of him. "If they don't hurry, we're going to be caught unprepared."

Tiger, Peter, and March all stand on the edge waiting for their daughter to come back out. Staring into Peter's face, he doesn't seem worried at all, as if he knows something the others don't. Only because of his expression do I relax. If he believes in his daughter, I can believe in my wolf.

Everything will be okay. It has to be.

The power inside the golden sphere flares brightly, making us all shield our eyes against it. I blink at the light, trying to see Red inside of it, but there's only brilliant power.

"Come on, little wolf," I whisper.

"*She'll be okay,*" Ophir murmurs in my mind, always believing in her. "*She always is.*"

"*She better be,*" Fang snarls. "*We can't lose her.*"

"We won't lose her," I say out loud. "We won't because I refuse."

I refuse. . .

CHAPTER FORTY-FOUR

JUPITER

My body feels alive, and what a strange thing to think about. I was alive before. How can I be more alive than I once was? And yet, that's how it feels. The pain still dances along my skin, the pinpricks that feel as if they should draw blood, but my skin remains unblemished. My stomach has calmed at least. A blessing among all the curses.

I'm sitting in the middle of some sort of power I neither understand nor want, but I know there's no option here. The power has chosen me, has decided that I'm to be the one who wields it. There's too much of it, though. It feels like there's too much to fit inside my body, but still somehow, I know it'll fit.

None of these thoughts can distract me from what I've done.

I hurt White, and I don't know how to unlock his mind.

"Find the stars," the wolf repeats from beside me. I don't know her name, but I can only assume she's the one Tin, Crow, and Briella went to retrieve. I feel no danger from her though her form should be terrifying. But I've seen worse creatures than a werewolf with magic. She doesn't scare me. I don't know her name, but I know her soul, our powers twisting together in familiarity.

I sit within this forcefield of power, my mate cradled in my lap, holding a stranger's hand. If someone long before I came to Wonderland told me this was my destiny, I would have laughed and asked them what sorts of drugs they were on. I'd longed for adventure, and I've gotten it and more. Now, I'd love a moment to simply enjoy White. Just a week. One day, I'll be able to sit with my mate and just. . .exist.

With my eyes closed, I do as Aniya and the wolf tell me. I sift through the power floating inside my body, trying to find the stars that are so important. The buzzing along my skin grows more intense the more I search for it, as if warning me of what I'm about to do. Still, I know without a doubt what my decision is going to be. I would die for White. If I have to change, to become, to save him, there's really no question.

I'll give him everything inside me if he'll only open his eyes.

"Find the stars," I whisper to myself, searching, searching, searching.

The sparks in my mind draw my attention, pull me to them, and I stare at them for far too long attempting to interpret the feeling they illicit in my body. I don't understand. Stars. I need to find the stars.

And then I feel it, the certainty that the sparks are the stars hovering around with nowhere to go, not yet. Inside my mind, they don't know where their destination is because I haven't accepted them. I'm afraid of them and so they don't burrow deep. But what happens if I do so? Will I be forever someone else? Will I still be me?

The magic curls around me in an almost hug, embracing me, asking for a chance, and the familiarity isn't lost on me.

"Our new powers are intertwined," I murmur, speaking to the wolf whose claws wrap around my fingers.

"Hansel and Gretel died," she replies, her voice just as soft. "Their magic has apparently chosen us to keep the balance."

My stomach drops. "Does that make us World Breakers?"

Hesitation, before she speaks again. "I don't think so. I don't feel like a World Breaker, but we're powerful. A balance, Crow said." She pauses. "Even if we were World Breakers, it wouldn't matter."

"Why?" I ask, pulling the power in closer, slowly accepting it. As I sit, the sparks begin to absorb into my mind, lighting my soul on fire without burning.

"Because we're good," she says, and there's so much certainty within those words, I believe them without question.

"Even with all this power?"

"Even with," she agrees.

The sparks sink further into my skin, falling inside, and I feel our bodies glow with it even with my eyes closed. My limbs strengthen. Something in my mind opens up, a lock released, something that's always been there but the power helps me to find. I was never only Jupiter, never just a Dreamwalker. I've always been more, and this moment has been meant to happen since the second I stepped into Wonderland.

Opening my eyes, I look at the wolf that feels like kin, and something inside me reaches out at feeling like a sibling again. Somehow, this power feels like there's a part of Neptune there, and I ache with that knowledge. Somewhere, my sister watches over me. I'm not religious, but I've seen too many things since I've left my world to think everyone simply dies and that's it.

I look down at White where he lays serenely in my lap. His ears twitch in agitation even as his eyes remain closed. I'd hurt him because I didn't understand, because I couldn't control it. I only hope he'll forgive me.

"Will you help me free him?" I ask the wolf, looking up into her eyes.

She nods and reaches her other hand forward, both of us moving on instinct. Against the orb, Aniya watches, not offering advice. She's already done plenty, telling us which direction to go. One day, Aniya will make the worlds shake, but it won't be a horrifying event. It'll bring good and peace.

Together, the wolf and I lay our hands on White's forehead. She's careful not to scratch him with her claws, just as I'm careful not to shift him too much. Gently, we both call forward our stars together, filling the sphere we sit in with the purple, green, and yellow sparks that dance in the air around us. Everything moves and swirls, both powers joining together as if we're one and the same. When there's enough of them, I push the stars toward White's mind, picturing a lock that needs opened.

The sphere around us gently pulls in before exploding around us in a burst of light and sparks, filling the sky with our power. Outside, the others stare in surprise at the suddenness of it, but they don't move, not yet.

"Wake up," I whisper to my rabbit, gently stroking his hair. "Wake up."

Aniya stands peacefully in the same spot. She hadn't moved when the power burst, didn't shield her eyes. She doesn't need to.

The light fades. The sparks pull back inside the two of us, and only then does the wolf release both me and White. She steps back and stands, giving us space.

White's eyes flicker before they pop open, and for a moment, those silver irises I love are ringed with the same fire I feel in my veins before it fades away and he looks like himself again.

A sob catches in my throat. "Hello, bunny," I whisper.

And then he's sitting up and wrapping strong arms around me, holding me so tightly, everything I was worried would shatter fuses back together stronger. The tears that fall along my cheeks burn a trail of stars there, glittering with their brightness. A problem for another time. I simply wrap my own arms around the White Rabbit and hold him until I can convince myself I'm not a monster.

I'm still Jupiter. I'm still me. I'm just a little brighter now.

My eyes trail around the circle to a now human woman, another redhead. I know she's the wolf because I can feel her power as she stands next to the Lion. "Thank you," I mouth to her.

With her gentle nod, I know things are going to be okay. We will be okay. We have to be.

The star dust in my breath demands it.

CHAPTER FORTY-FIVE

RED

I watch closely as everyone surrounds Jupiter and White, checking on them, worried. I know they're okay because of the stars. Jupiter and I are linked in some way. It's only fitting that be both carry the same fire in our veins as we do in our hair color. I wonder if I should explain to Jupiter what exactly her power told me, if she understands fully what she's become, but I figure it's a conversation for after her friends speak to her. They were all so worried.

My eyes trail over to Aniya where Tiger, Peter, and March all fawn around her, checking to make sure she's okay. Peter seems to be unworried, his eyes tracing over her to affirm what he already knows. When his eyes meet mine with gratitude, I get a sense for the same stars that we carry, as if he has a small portion inside his own body. It shouldn't surprise me, but I still blink. Of course Aniya would carry so much. A bridge into the power came from her own father.

All the creatures that Aniya is rarely seen without flock to her side, including what someone calls a Lost Boy. Really, it looks like a man with great horns, more beastly than human, but still a creature just the same. He and the other creatures take up their spots of protection and check her over, reassuring themselves she's okay. I'd hate to think what they'd do should she not be.

King stands at my side, his fingers intertwined with mine again. When I'd come out, he'd immediately pulled me into a hug despite still being a wolf. As we'd embraced, I'd slowly shifted back to human form, absorbing his warmth into my skin. Now, he stands shirtless, the fabric gifted to me yet again.

"That one is powerful,' I say, gesturing to Aniya.

King nods. "That's why they suspect she's a World Breaker."

I study her closely. "She's chosen to be good."

"Because she's been raised with love and care. Her potential for evil is there, just as all of us have. But Aniya cares for people in this world. She will not break it, but she will make it tremble one day at her feet."

"It's just which side we foster," I murmur. "How many of us need to be reminded of that very sentiment?"

King's eyes meet mine. "All of us, little wolf." And then he smiles and something inside me begs to tell him, to explain exactly how I feel. I know with certainly what this is. I'd questioned what I felt once in my life and had suffered for it. Now, I know I need to speak my truth.

I open my mouth just as Emerald City explodes in a beam of light behind us. We all duck at the explosion that rocks Oz, at the blast of power that spreads out from the castle in the distance. The flying monkeys that had been swirling above it in a vortex direct themselves up and out, spreading out over Oz, heading in our direction. We all watch with wide eyes, knowing there's no more time for planning. It's time to act.

Tin swears and drags a hand through his hair. "It's time," he grunts. "Is everyone ready?"

There's the sound of water hitting the ground, and as one, we all look toward Clara where she stands with her eyes wide. I stare in horror at the wetness on the ground, understand what exactly it means. Her hand is on her stomach in shock, but she doesn't move.

Hatter stares with eyes so wide, there's more white than gold. "Oh fuck. Oh, wonder! What do I do? What do we do?" His hands go to his head and hold in horror. "What the fuck do we do?"

Everyone begins to panic at once. The flying monkeys are on their way to attack. Toto and Ananke are probably doing the same. And now Clara is going into labor.

Cinder sighs where she stands. "Let's add that to the list of problems, shall we?"

CHAPTER FORTY-SIX

HATTER

The madness inside me strokes to life at my pure panic. I've known this day would come, but I hoped it would be after the fight, had hoped we'd have time to save Oz and make Clara comfortable before she has the baby.

"Hatter," she gasps, reaching for me, and despite my panic, I immediately scoop her into my arms and cradle her against me. No mate of mine is going to walk while in labor. Not on my watch!

I need to get her somewhere safe. My eyes drift to the flying creatures headed our way and I know what's about to happen. Clara was never going to be part of this fight but with this happening, we're going to lose people who could have helped. With long strides, I rush toward Tin's home and go inside.

Panic sings in my soul but I shove it down. Clara needs strength right now, not panic.

She keens in my arms, her fingers clutching tightly in my coat as whatever pain hits her. My heart throbs painfully in my chest.

"What's wrong? What is it?" I growl, not knowing how to help.

"It's only a contraction," Jupiter answers, rushing in behind me. Tiger is on her heels, the only two women I trust to help my mate. Tiger has birthed before. Jupiter is smart enough to know the science behind it. This is the best we can do. No one else knows what's happening.

"She's in pain," I rasp in frustration, gently lying her down on a bed. Her fingers immediately thread with mine and squeeze so hard, I actually feel my bones pop.

"Childbirth is painful," Tiger reminds me.

"And we have no drugs to counter the pain," Jupiter adds. "We're going natural here."

I don't really understand what she's talking about. I know she'd once mentioned there are drugs in her world to help with childbirth but there was no way to get them, not with everything going on. I don't know what a natural birth means though. I don't know what I can do to help.

"You need to go fight," Clara growls up at me. "They need you."

But I ignore her order. Now isn't the time.

The madness whispers in my soul and spills from my lips.

"What do we do? How can I help? I don't know where to begin. Give me direction and help me help, so that I can help my empress," I say.

Tiger looks at me strangely, but Jupiter doesn't even react. So long ago, Jupiter remembers what it was like before my madness dissipated. Tiger has never seen me spit out rhymes without reason. I don't waste time explaining. Instead, I offer my hand for Clara to squeeze again as another high keen comes from her lips.

My body buzzes with emotions, stress eating at my heart. My mate is in pain, and I can't help her!

"Breathe," Tiger tells Clara as I grimace with her hold on my hand. "You need to breathe, Clara."

My mate immediately begins to breathe in the way she and Tiger had practiced before. I'd walked in on them discussing what to expect. The hold on my hand eases.

"That's it," Jupiter encourages. "You're doing great, Clara. We're going to do this together. Tiger here knows what it's like to have a baby and I've seen a lot of movies and documentaries."

My eyes widen. That doesn't sound promising. They need to know what they're doing! I open my mouth to say so, to let more madness tumble out, but Clara grips my fingers in another death grip and I breathe through the pain as one of the bones in my hand breaks. I don't want her to worry, don't want her to realize she's hurting me. My mate needs my strength and if broken bones are my way of helping, then so be it. They'll heal anyway.

Jupiter's hair is wild as she turns and grabs a towel. She wets it in the vanity before lying it across Clara's now sweat-soaked forehead. I should have done that. I should be taking care of her. I move to help but Clara's hand won't release me, keeping me close.

"It's about to get real personal," Jupiter warns Clara before she tosses Clara's skirt up over her knees. "How far apart are the contractions? You're starting to dilate I think," she murmurs, staring at Clara's nether regions.

"What do you mean 'think'?" I growl. "You're a scientist! You're supposed to know!" I don't mean for the outburst to hit me, but it tumbles out before I can stop it. I'm panicked and I know it. I'm losing control of my emotions.

Jupiter looks at me with fire ringing her eyes, panic equally there. She's just as freaked out as I am. There is new power circulating in her veins. She's left her mate outside to fight. Both Tiger and she have left those they care about outside to help my mate.

"A scientist, yes!" she screams back. "I'm not a labor doctor!"

"Enough!" Clara growls, her teeth grinding together as another contraction hits her. She starts to breathe through it. We all wait for her to speak again, not interrupting her process. "Everyone needs to calm down. We have a job to do." She looks up at me. "Hatter, you need to get outside and help the fight."

"I'm not leaving you," I snarl.

Strong fingers curl into my coat and jerk me down, Clara's strength greater than I remember as I nearly tumble on top of her. I just barely catch myself.

"Our friends are going into battle to save the worlds, Hatter. They need you," she grunts, her face twisted with pain.

"But so do you!"

"I'll be fine," she groans. "Just get out there and save the world so our baby has somewhere to live."

I glance at Jupiter and Tiger, torn between listening to my mate and staying to make sure she's okay. The thought of leaving her in this vulnerable position makes my stomach sick but she's right. If we don't win this war, there won't be a world for our baby to grow up in.

"We've got this," Jupiter reassures me. "Once you leave, I'll put a sphere around the room, so we're all protected."

"You can do that?" I ask, knowing her powers had been erratic before. Now, I can feel the power in her veins, know she's different, so I'm not surprised when she snaps her fingers, and a force field snaps into place around us. She snaps those fingers again and it disappears, as easy as blinking. "Never mind."

"Go," Clara urges. "Help them!" She starts keening again as another contraction hits her.

"We'll keep her safe," Tiger promises. "Both of them."

I look between the two women helping my Clara Bee and my chest tightens. Quickly, I lean down and press a kiss against my mate's forehead. When I go to pull away, she pulls me back down for a kiss on her lips. There's passion and love there, a little bit of fear, and everything we've ever been through together. This is just another adventure. My mate is strong and the women with her are equally so. She'll be okay. I refuse to believe otherwise.

"I'm leaving only because I must," I murmur, kissing her again. "Stay safe, my empress, my Clara Bee. I would perish upon this very realm if you were to ever leave me."

Clara, despite her pain, squeezes my fingers tightly one more time and releases them. "Stay safe, my Hatter, my everything. If you die, I'll bring you back," she begins to grunt again, but finishes her rhyme despite it. "and kill you myself again."

I smile widely at her and press one more quick kiss against her forehead. Stepping back, I nod to Jupiter who snaps, and the protective bubble appears between us. With one last look at my mate inside struggling to give birth to our child, I rush back outside just in time to catch the first wave of flying monkeys descending on Gillikin City.

CHAPTER FORTY-SEVEN

RED

The flying monkeys swarm Gillikin City like a herd of banshees intent on crushing it. They fly straight into buildings and attack Tin's people with teeth sharper than daggers. I watch as one of the creatures lifts an angry man with a metal arm high into the air before dropping him. I wince at the sound, but shift into my wolf quickly, shredding through the shirt King had given me yet again.

"Red! Catch!" Briella shouts, tossing something heavy toward me.

I just barely catch it and grunt under its weight before I realize it's armor. Not only armor, but armor that fits my wolf form and covers my chest. A design is stamped into the heavy material, or sewn maybe. I don't have the skill of recognition when it comes to fabric. But the design, I can see clearly, and I have to blink my eyes quickly to clear any emotion.

It's a crest, a wolf and a lion emblazoned on it, rearing toward each other.

"It'll shift with you to fit your human form," she shouts even as she swings an axe above her head and violently takes out a flying monkey. I watch as she slams the axe into its head over and over again until it stops moving. Then with a violent battle cry that makes Tin laugh beside her, she rushes back into the fight alongside her mate.

Quickly pulling on the armor, I buckle it in place just in time for one of the flying monkeys to target me.

The creatures are horrid. Though the thought of them should be cute in theory, they're anything but. Their furred bodies look like some mishmash of a primate and a demon. Roughly the shape of a primate, that's where the similarities end. Their fur is patchy and rough, as if its been worn away by decay. Sharp teeth fill their mouths in rows that you see as they screech at you. Black, leathery wings come from their backs and flap erratically.

The flying monkey that thinks it can take me on is missing a foot. It's a strange detail to notice just before I slice it in half with my claws, cutting off its shrill battle cry. Black blood splatters my coat but I pay it no mind. Battles are messy. I have no doubt I'll be covered in blood by the end of this.

"We need to find Toto and Ananke," Azalea shouts from where she fights alongside Wolfbane. Wolfbane wears his crocodile skin and if he wasn't on our side, I'd be terrified of him. I've never seen a creature quite like that, especially not one that snaps the flying monkeys in two with his jaws. Of course, that's until I see Flam shift into his form and my eyes widen further. What allies we've made in this war!

"Why?" I shout back when no one answers her.

"We take them out, this all stops. The flying monkeys only attack when controlled."

I'm amazed at the powers in our group and suddenly feel confident in our chances. We are many. We are strong.

Young Aniya stands in the midst of the fight, not lifting a finger as her creatures keep her safe, swarming around her. If they didn't, then Peter and March on either side of her would ensure she wasn't hurt. Peter fights with his bare hands, laughter trickling out of his mouth at the killing. He enjoys it too much to be considered wholly good, but something tells me Peter once danced in the darkness more than he does in the light. March swings a great silver sword in an arc around him, slicing flying monkeys in two that make it passed Peter.

On another side of them, Hook and Wendy swirl their hands in circles, and I watch in surprise as their powers form. Water swirls around Wendy and drowns the creatures while they fly. The wind breaks their wings and drops them to the earth—Hook's doing—where Wendy's water finishes the job. They're a single unit. Water and air. Ocean and Horizon. A better pairing couldn't have been made if the cosmos tried.

Atlas and Tink fight with their backs together, both sporting deadly looking claws. Though Tink still looks the same, glittering dust dances around her and lifts her slightly into the air with her movements, an action she doesn't seem to realize she's doing. That dust almost looks like wings if you look at it just right. Atlas, with skin dark blue and covered with glowing golden symbols, stands as a beast I don't recognize. With a furious growl, he shreds the enemies as if they're no more than paper.

Hatter, White, Cheshire, and Cal all fight together as a unit. Hatter, White, and Cal swing brutal looking swords around them, cutting a path. Cheshire is completely covered in fur, a closer creature to my own that brutally cuts the creatures. His tail swipes back and forth in aggression.

The Flamingo and the Dodo bird destroy the creatures by the dozens, and if they weren't on our side, I'd run screaming from the two of them as they work together. A massive black dragon-like creature with pink feathers, Flam should be silly, but he's far more terrifying for it as he swirls around like a giant snake. Doe is mostly featherless in her bird form. She's massive and heavily scarred, her great beak snapping at the flying monkeys that dare get too close.

Cinder and Crow stand still in the middle of our group, powers swirling between the two of them. Neither has to move as lime green and pink power leech from them and fall the flying monkeys as if by magic alone.

And finally, King, my own mate, stands beside me with his own claws as he shreds the creatures to pieces. He hasn't shifted, hasn't shown me his lion, but he's no less brutal for it. He doesn't have to shift to cut the creatures from the sky. His furious growl resonates inside my bones.

A howl breaks the air around us and it isn't from me. The flying monkeys go into a frenzy, attacking our group and Tin's people violently, as if whatever's coming makes them both angry and brutal.

"Here they come," King warns.

I turn just in time to see the woman first, Ananke, the World Breaker everyone has been warning about. She comes around the street corner, the flying monkeys avoiding her like she's plagued by disease. Wearing a soft pink dress and golden hair flowing around her shoulders, she's beautiful. Someone intent on destroying the worlds should be ugly, but fate rarely has such a sense of humor. Evil always appears innocent and ethereal. It always gives the impression of good before it does bad.

I'm wondering at the strangeness of it until my eyes catch and hold on the creature following along behind her, at the hulking beast that bleeds with magic so very like my own.

I freeze where I stand and without thinking, my bones begin to snap quickly, leaving me standing in human flesh, vulnerable, but the flying monkeys aren't focusing on me right now. They're focusing on Tin's people, leaving the rest of us to face the true threats.

King panics beside me, taking up position to protect me in my human form. "What are you doing? Red!" he growls, swiping at a flying monkey that gets too close. "Shift back!"

But I'm staring at the great wolf creature beside the woman, at eyes that are so familiar, my entire body revolts against the sight of them. He stares right back at me and everything in the background fades to nothing as horror freezes my heart inside my chest.

"Perry?" I breath.

Toto, the lobo I know I need to fight, tilts his head toward me before he bares his teeth in a great toothy grin. "Hello," he purrs. ". . .Scarlett."

King's eyes widen beside me just as White dances by with his sword. "How is that possible?" my lion asks.

"Time moves differently in every world," White answers as he passes by. "Everything's possible."

But I'm still staring at the wolf of my nightmares, at the man who I'd trusted before he'd dug his teeth into my shoulder and destroyed my entire world. "I killed you," I rasp, remembering vividly the moment I'd plunged a silver dagger into his heart.

He grins and focuses completely on me, far more interested in me than any of the other fighting. Ananke looks between us in amusement before moving toward the group of others, her eyes on their defensive stances.

"You tried to kill me," Toto corrects. "But I escaped. A helpful young woman named Dorothy unknowingly gave me some of her life force so that I could live." He takes a step toward us and King growls savagely in warning. The other wolf pays him no mind. "And I no longer go by the name Perry, my sweet Scarlett. I'm Toto."

And then he lunges toward me, but I'm frozen by the past, every bad memory coming to the forefront of my mind.

Perry, what big teeth you have. . .

CHAPTER FORTY-EIGHT

I watch as Toto's great teeth get closer and closer to me and still, I can't move. The past and the present collide and freeze my body, making it impossible to move, to fight, to run. I can't do anything and no matter how hard I tell my body to do something, anything, it won't listen.

Before Toto can swallow me whole or rip me to shreds, just when I think I'm about to die, King is there, slamming into Toto with the full force of his power. The wolf and the Lion go tumbling head over heels, slashing at each other with savage growls. When I see the smear of blood on King's side, I snarl, breaking free from my trauma-induced trance.

No one touches my Lion!

I shift without thinking, my fingers lengthening into claws, and I leap forward, slashing at Toto violently to protect King. The two break apart, rolling away to catch their bearing, and I jerk King to his feet before he can himself.

"Now would be a good time to shift," I growl, rolling my shoulders. Blood drips from my claws where I'd cut them along Toto's side. I take pleasure in seeing the liquid stain his coat, in hurting the man that once ruined my life.

King doesn't answer, but when Toto lunges forward again, I hear the first sounds of bones popping beside me. I move to meet Toto's lunge, prepared to fight him until I have nothing left. Violet sparks fly from my shoulders and slam forward, making the other wolf smile with glee.

"You're just like me, Scarlett. I knew you were special," he purrs as we slam together.

I slash at him, but he doesn't even raise a claw toward me, laughter tumbling from his lips as I cut. And then the violent roar fills the air behind us, and we both turn in surprise to search for the source.

Stumbling away from Toto at the sight before me, I stare in wonder at the beast King becomes when he's free of his human flesh.

I expected a lion. I'm sure everyone expected a simple, large lion, but that isn't what I see. King isn't just a lion. He's a three-headed lion. King, Ophir, and Fang all roar as one, a warning to Toto not to touch me, and all I can do is stare at the gloriousness that is my mate.

"What is this?" Toto hisses. "You've found yourself another beast to protect you." His lips curl up in a snarl. "You're mine!"

Three lion heads peel back their lips at the wolf. "She belongs to no one but herself!" King growls, and then he's lunging forward to meet Toto in a deadly fight filled with slashing claws and snapping teeth. A few of the others stare at them with wide eyes but they're too preoccupied with their own fight with Ananke as she begins to throw magic at them. That magic cracks the earth beneath her feet, as if not even the ground can withstand her power.

I leap into the fight, slashing at Toto until his blood drips to the stone, feeding the yellow brick beneath our feet. Azalea and Croc come over to help us, throwing their own strengths into the mix. There's a split second where we all break apart, and Toto doesn't wait for either of us to grab him. Instead, he swipes his claws at Azalea, cutting her belly open with a savage snarl of, "the witch who imprisoned me!". Wolfbane catches her before she falls, gently setting her on the ground as King and I attack the wolf again, all snarling our hate and anger. I want him to die! I want him to not exist in this world ever again.

With a violent howl, power explodes out of me, the sparks coming to life and arrowing into Toto like spikes. He howls in pain as they pierce his hide, and he turns to me, his own magic coming forth and swirling at me, but I'm not just Red anymore. I'm Feral, and I am angry.

We meet in a clash that rocks the world, our claws tearing at each other savagely, our magic fighting for dominance, lobo against lobo, past against present.

"I'm going to kill you," I spit as I dig my claws into his side.

"So savage," he purrs back. "I can't wait to make you my queen."

King snarls behind me and I hear Fang and Ophir shouting words, but I'm focused on the wolf before me. I don't know what they're saying.

"I've never been yours," I say, and his eyes narrow in anger. "And I never will be."

"We'll see about that, Scarlett," he growls as he blocks one of my swings. "We'll see about that."

CHAPTER FORTY-NINE

CINDER

We all fight against the magic swirling around us, desperately trying to get to the woman who wields magic stronger than almost anything I've seen before. The ground cracks beneath her feet as she lifts her fingers and pink, innocent looking magic spears into us, hurting, harming, slicing our skin. There's so many of us focused on her and yet we don't make progress, not even will all the power we throw at her. Flam and Doe are off fighting the flying monkeys, trying to help Tin's people who are at a disadvantage in power. King and Red fight against Toto, both savagely trying to take down the World Breaker who once cut through Oz. Azalea is down, Croc trying to stop her bleeding desperately, digging through her bag for bottles that she weakly directs him to find. The rest of us are using our own magic to fight against Ananke, this woman who was once forced to sleep for the danger she poses to the worlds.

"Pitiful," Ananke laughs, throwing her hands wide for more power to roll from. "You don't stand a chance. Your bones will grind to dust and add to the ashes of this world."

Tin snarls and throws an axe at her. I watch in surprise as it freezes in the air before her. With a giggle, the axe crumbles to dust. "Nice try, metal man, but it won't be that easy to kill me."

There's another axe in Tin's hand a moment later.

There's so much going on around me, I can't focus on anything more than the woman in front of us, powerful beyond compare, and still, with so many, we can't seem to gain any ground. We're powerful, and yet still at a disadvantage.

Wendy grunts in pain as something spears into her shoulder. The pirate captain doesn't stop fighting but Hook savagely tries to hurt Ananke for daring to harm his mate. The violent tornado of power he throws at her barely does more than lift her hair.

Another bolt has the White Rabbit going down, his thigh oozing blood where a spear of power stabbed. With a snarl of pain, he drags himself back to his feet and somehow puts his weight on the leg, some sort of healing that feels as if it should move faster. That, or he holds himself upright with pure willpower alone.

With a sudden realization, I understand we could very well lose this fight. Despite all our power, despite our strength, we could still lose. We need the others inside, but Clara is in the process of giving birth, Tiger and Jupiter doing their best to help. They can't come out. King and Red are indisposed while they fight the creature that once decimated Oz and still somehow, they hold their own simply because of the woman who had pulled Jupiter from her own mind. Purple sparks glitter dangerously around them, attacking Toto like angry fireflies.

My eyes widen and I look first to Red and then to Aniya where she stands in the midst of the fighting, not lifting a finger as she watches. Her creatures swirl around her, fighting off the magic thrown their way, keeping her protected even as she stands out here. She should be inside with Clara, protected, but instead, she stands out here. . .

. . .as if she knows precisely where to be.

"The stars!" I gasp. "Crow, the stars!"

Crow looks over at me in confusion and the distraction is all the power needs to spear into his chest. I scream, rushing over to him, but he waves me away.

"I'm fine," he grunts. "It'll heal in a moment. It just hurts like a bitch."

My face scrunching up in anger, I turn to the woman before me. Her magic and mine hold a similar color but I don't have the stars Red has. Still, I'm strong, the powers my mother passed to me swelling with my anger. With a scream, my head tips back and the magic blasts from inside me, slamming into Ananke with a brutal shove that actually has her stumbling back. Arms wide open, I let my power keep hitting her like a succession of punches. The others join in, making her stumble back another step, all of our powers hitting at once. As one, we give everything we have, until I feel my power stutter. I'm strong, but the power is still new. It's finite, and when the pink smoke disappears, I open my eyes to see Ananke straighten roughly and glare at us.

My stomach sinks.

Her eyes narrow. "I grow tired of these games," she snarls, and with a wave of her hand, my body freezes, all except for my eyes. I glance around to see almost everyone else is frozen, too, all but Aniya.

Ananke walks up to me and Crow fights against the bonds that hold him, desperate to get to me, but the woman is too strong. We're going to lose. Fuck, we're going to lose!

The stars! My eyes trail over to Aniya who remains unfrozen, her hands folded primly before her, waiting.

Ananke caresses my cheek. "You're powerful, but still new," she murmurs. "You could have been great."

Power trickles from my body and snaps out at her, biting at her touch until she pulls her hand away. *Don't fucking touch me!* I snarl in my mind, and her lips curl as if she can hear me.

"So strong," she purrs and dismisses me, turning toward Aniya and I tense even more. Despite my theory, she's still a child, barely a young woman. And no one else can move. Fuck! I push against the power and my pinky moves, just barely. I have to get out. I have to help!

"Hello, little World Breaker," Ananke purrs to Aniya. "Would you like to break the world with me?" She offers her hand to Aniya and the young woman stares at her palm a few seconds before she looks back up into her face, unafraid.

"No, thank you," Aniya says with a smile. "I rather like the people living in it."

Someone growls. Peter. His arm moves as he fights against the hold, but Ananke doesn't notice. More stars. Behind me, I hear Red shift against the power holding her seconds from gutting Toto. Stars!

All the stars. Looking deep inside me, I search for my power, stroke it, beckon it. We need more stars.

"They'll break your heart in the end," Beauty warns Aniya, not noticing the struggle going on around her. She's strong, but we've been given all that we need to. The answer is in the stars.

"Heartbreak is inevitable," Aniya agrees. "But that doesn't mean evil should win."

Ananke tilts her head and studies Aniya as if she's a creature she can't quite understand. "So, you think I'm evil then?" she coos, playing a game I know she won't win. Aniya is strong, the strongest of us all. She's not frozen because she wills it so, not because Ananke chose for her not to be.

Aniya just shakes her head. "Not evil," she says, and there's a weight to her words that speaks not only of power, but of prophesy. "Just hurt." In the distance, a baby cries, but it's not coming from Tin's home where Clara labors. It comes from the Grimm Forest. "Just *hurt*," Aniya repeats.

Ananke's eyes widen and she stumbles back in horror. Her power releases everyone at once and Red snarls behind me. Everyone moves at the same time, moving to seize the opportunity. We all rush toward Ananke, but Cal is there first, her mighty sword raised in preparation to take her head.

"Not yet," Aniya commands, and Cal stops, her brows furrowed in confusion.

The sound of a crying baby grows louder, and Hatter looks around, as if worried his own soon-to-be child is out there. When he realizes the same thing I do, his shoulders tense further and he looks out into the Grimm forest, following all our gaze.

Ananke, her eyes wide in panic and pain as the sounds of the baby grow louder, turns and rushes off into the forest after the sound, following it. I'd seen the desperation in her eyes before she's taken off, had felt her pain.

We all watch in shock before giving hesitant chase.

"What's happening?" I growl, following them.

"I don't know," Crow replies, his eyes wide just as mine are. "I don't know."

CHAPTER FIFTY

RED

Claw marks down my back drip red drops of blood onto the yellow brick beneath my feet, trickling over my fur. It's a manageable injury, one I barely pay any mind to. The sparks swirl around me, leaking from my skin. I know they can heal me, but I hold them off for now. First, we destroy Toto. Then we heal.

Behind us, Azalea is seriously hurt, the witch bleeding out at a rapid rate. In any other world, she would have been a lost cause, but Croc works quickly to mix things from a bag at her side, dumping one thing after another onto the gaping wound in Azalea's stomach. Every time I glance back to check on them, the wound is a little better looking, a slow process but a welcome one. Wolfbane is sporting his own injury, a chunk missing from his hide that will need to be healed but it's clear he's not paying attention to his own injuries in favor of saving his woman.

King stands beside me, a massive beast that I never expected. He's even more beautiful in this form, all three of the men I've taken into my soul represented. He's larger than I am in my wolf form, and had he not been on my side, I would have most definitely been terrified at the sight of him.

Toto's eyes glance between us, seeing the clear connection. His muzzle curls up in a savage snarl that stinks of jealousy, which is funny to me. How dare he be jealous when he'd never offered me anything more than nightmares? Of course, he probably doesn't even realize his twisted notions. We once planned to get married. Now, nothing could ever make me look at him as anything other than a monster too lost to be saved.

With a snarl fit for a demon, I lunge forward at the same time King does, my magic snapping out toward Toto mercilessly. His own magic rises to meet mine, stopping it from penetrating his fur, but I still smell the telltale sizzle of burning hair, as if my magic singes his coat. The wolf dodges King's maw but doesn't avoid my claws. With a brutal blow, I drag them down his shoulder, a near identical wound to the one I once gave King on our first meeting.

Toto doesn't get angry. Instead, he grins and backs away, putting us back into the circle. We all stalk each other like the predators we are. This isn't a battle that can be won with anything other than monsters and beasts.

"My, what a pretty monster you've become," Toto coos to me. "I made the right decision to keep you."

My eyes narrow in annoyance. "What happened to the Perry I knew?" I ask, moving around. I'm panting just a little from the blood loss, but otherwise, I feel stronger than ever.

Toto's grins. "He died the day you ran a silver blade through my chest."

I had hoped he died, had thought using silver was enough, but apparently, whoever Dorothy was, she was strong enough to save him whether she wanted to or not. Another woman fooled by Perry's charm. I realize now he was never just kind, never nice. He was manipulative, sure, and when he became a wolf, that characteristic trait was only heightened. Now he stands before me a completely different being. He's right. I killed the Perry I knew. This is a different beast.

"I did so because of what you'd become," I offer, staring at him. King moves beside me, letting me take the lead on this, waiting for me to rush him so he can join me. "You killed my mother," I remind him.

With the words out of my mouth, it brings forward the imagery that still haunts my nightmares, but I push them aside. I'm more than my trauma. Perry will no longer rule my life, one way or the other. If it takes everything in me, I'll heal with my friends by my side. It won't be anything quick—healing takes time—but at least I have someone willing to stand beside me while I work through them. I glance over at King, knowing he, Ophir, and Fang will stand with me through everything, the new powers, the trauma, the healing, the love. We will conquer it all together.

The love.

"I did it for you," Toto growls. "I freed you."

Anger fills me. "You made me into a monster incapable of accepting that I was a monster!" I swipe my claws out in warning. "You gave me nothing but pain!"

"But look at how beautiful you are," he purrs. "You'll make a nice mate."

King's rumbling growl fills the air around us. "She's already spoken for," he spits, his muzzle peeling back. Fang and Ophir makes sounds of fury, a warning and a promise.

"We're going to fucking destroy you," Fang warns from beside him, the second lion head looking far more savage than I've ever given him credit for. I know Fang is by far the more brutal of the three, but seeing him with his own face, with his own actions, I realize exactly how he is. Fang will destroy anyone he desires, and he has his sights set on the lobo before us.

Ophir roars from the other side, the sound shaking the ground beneath my feet as he announces his feelings on the matter.

As one, we both leap forward to slam into Toto, wrestling between us, fighting to gain the upper hand. I don't know how King can stomach being in the midst of our magic as it fights to gain ground, but he doesn't buckle, doesn't back down. If anything, my magic only seems to spur him on even while Toto's magic bites at him.

And then Toto's magic slams into King fully and digs in, ripping wounds open all over King's hide and dropping his blood to the road. He roars in pain and rears back, great swiping claws reaching for Toto. I hear his pain, see the evidence of it, and something inside of me shifts. I was a monster before. Now, I'm something more.

I see red as King jerks away to gather himself. He's limping, one of his legs at a strange angle, and the wounds along his body bleed profusely. With my teeth bared, I turn back to Toto, eerily calm. Sparks swarm from my shoulders and circle me, spreading wide, showing my true power. Toto watches both in awe and a little bit in fear, but there's nothing inside of me that feels anything for the asshole he's become. This is my world now. Now one is going to destroy it.

All the lives I've taken, all the lives Toto has, they're all because of Perry. They're all because of this lobo who dares to claim me as his own. But I will not be claimed. I belong to myself. I am the wild and the wolf. I am the storm no one expects. A wolf will never be a pet.

"We're both monsters," Toto snarls at me, as if to remind me of what I am, but it's a pointless plea.

"Yes," I agree, taking a step toward him with my teeth bared. "But I chose to be a better monster."

And with a savage howl that speaks to the horrors of what I've done, I lunge for his jugular.

CHAPTER FIFTY-ONE

FANG

Pain bites into my body, spreads through our veins as Toto's magic continues to worm its way inside. I would itch at the wounds if not for the leg out of commission. We're already balancing on three legs as it is. If I itch, we're going down, and as an Heir, we cannot show such weakness.

"She's going in for the kill," Ophir growls. "We should help her."

"I'm going to rip him to shreds," I snarl, urging us forward, but King stops us.

"No," he replies, stalling our feet. "She doesn't need us. Watch."

As three, we all stare as Red howls a sound that would make any monster proud and lunges at the other lobo, a beast we hadn't been able to beat last time. We weren't strong enough then. We didn't have Red then.

"She's glorious," I whisper as she slams her claws through Toto's chest, digging in deep, making the other beast howl in pain. The same moment her claws make contact, her power slams inside the wound, making it glow with her sparks as it fills the cavity and spreads outward, destroying everything that he is, killing her demon.

"She's come full circle," Ophir comments. "She's ending a cycle of nightmares by killing the very creature that caused them."

King nods. "She knows exactly who she is now."

"Ours," I growl, shaking out my mane. "She's ours and we're hers."

"It's about time," Tin says from beside us suddenly and we nearly jump. I never even heard him walk up. "I always knew you were hiding something. I can't say I expected it to be three very separate minds, but it suits you." His eyes trail over to where Red continues to slash at Toto, ripping him apart piece by piece, her power swarming around each piece and setting it on fire. "Just as she suits you."

King glances at the woman who I know will change everything. "She's something, isn't she?"

Tin nods. "Briella likes her, but you should come with us. Ananke took off into the woods after Aniya spoke to her. We need to track her down."

We nod as one. "Go. We'll be right behind you, as soon as Red finishes Toto."

Tin stares at Red again. "It seems like so long ago when we were unable to finish him and yet it took only a single person."

"The universe provides what we need when we need it," Ophir says, repeating Tink's words. She was right. This is the moment Red was needed and so she came along precisely when the universe asked her to. Lobo against Lobo. She was always meant to battle beside me.

Tin doesn't wait for more words. Instead, he turns and takes off after the others, giving chase after the woman causing all the trouble. I listen for him leave, take notice as the flying monkeys begin to withdraw, signaling that Toto no longer has control of them. When I look at Red again, I realize it's because he's no longer breathing. Red has killed him, and still she slashes and splatters blood, spitting angry words with each strike.

"Wow," I breathe, and I feel the knowledge settle into all our minds. "So this is what it feels like."

King smiles. "Love is a strange thing, isn't it?"

With a hobble and a limp that's already starting to heal, we step forward. "Red," King calls, but she doesn't seem to hear him.

"Scarlett," I try. Nothing.

"Little wolf," Ophir purrs and she pauses mid strike. "He's dead and gone. Come. We have need to finish the other one."

She's covered in the blood of her enemy, the vibrant hue mixing with her own blood. As we watch, Toto's power leeches from his body and absorbs into the yellow brick below it, off to search for another source, but it doesn't go into Red. She's already powerful enough as she is.

"You're sure?" she asks, looking down at the final burning remnants of Toto. "He can't come back this time?"

"We're sure," King answers. "His power is leaving, and the flying monkeys are retreating. Toto is no more. Nothing can bring him back now."

The sparks around her move to the wound on her back, healing the large gash there, and as we watch, those same sparks come over to us and dance along our skin.

"What are you doing?" I ask, watching as a spark lands in a cut and warmth spreads outward from it. It's comforting, no bite of pain at all in the power. The small wound heals a second later and my eyes widen.

"She's healing us," Ophir offers, as if I hadn't already realized that.

More sparks land all along our body and heal each wound, a group of them going to our leg. With a painful snap, it straightens out, but the warmth eases the momentary pain. A few minutes later, we stand before her, completely healed, as if we'd not even battled at all.

"Let's go hunting," Red growls, her eyes on the Grimm Forest. "We have a job to finish."

Excitement fills me and my lips open before I can stop them. "One day, I'm going to make you our Queen."

Her eyes light up with amusement and she runs a blood-covered, clawed hand through my mane. "Do I get a crown?"

"The best crown," I purr. "You can wear it and only it while I fuck you next time."

Laughter tumbles out. "We'll discuss that more later."

And then together, we both shoot into the trees after the others, in search of the sleeping beauty who had caused so much trouble in our world.

CHAPTER FIFTY-TWO

RED

W e gain on the others quickly though they'd had a head start on us. With a howl, I announce our presence and the others pump their fists in the air along with us. Toto is dead. The monster that once haunted Oz is gone.

"You're a fucking ninja," Briella shouts at me, her eyes alight with the hunt.

I don't know what a ninja is, but I take it as the compliment she clearly means it as. Her armor still clings to me, now covered in blood, but no less worn for wear. She has excellent craftmanship and I know, though she's human, it's one of her powers. Somehow, Oz gave her exactly what she needed to do things as she does. No one escapes these worlds without some sort of power in their veins.

We expect to have to hunt the woman through the trees, that she'll keep running from us, but we break through the trees into Quadling Country to see her kneeling at the base of the crumbling castle she once slept in. Her pink dress is stained with dirt as she kneels there in the mud, her head bowed down in defeat. But no one had even harmed her. She sports no wounds, and she clearly has all her powers. Why would someone so powerful give up?

A baby crying echoes around the trees, and she flinches where she sits. I look around for the source, thinking maybe Clara had her baby, but Briella shakes her head.

"It's a phantom," she offers as explanation, as if it'll clear up all the answers but it only raises more questions for me.

The phantom of what?

We all surround her, unsure if she's going to fight or simply stay there. I'm confused, and I know most of us are the same. Only Aniya seems content and unworried as if she knows exactly what's going to happen. She probably does. As the most powerful person in this clearing, perhaps, she knows more than she's told anyone.

Aniya moves as I watch her and every single one of us tense. I frown when she walks up to Crow. With a gentle tug on his arm, she asks him to lean down so she can whisper something in his ear. Despite my advanced hearing, I can't catch the words she tells him that cause him to blink wide eyes at her.

"You're sure?" he asks.

Aniya nods up at him and he starts to swirl his fingers in the air.

As one, we all watch the mist that begins to roll into the clearing, but that isn't what we all focus on. It's the haze of a green soul that slowly dances along the air, moving toward the woman where she kneels. Ananke looks up at the soul, tears rolling from her eyes as she holds out her arms. I'm not the only one who gasps when the soul lands gently in her embrace and she cradles it close. When the soul takes the shape of a baby, I literally take a step back in confused horror. What is this?

Ananke strokes a finger through the hazy image, sobs wracking her chest. Pain. So much pain rolls from her shoulders, I almost can't take it.

I shift the same time as King does, our hands latching onto each other's as we witness this. Around the clearing, those in different forms do the same. This isn't a war. Not this time. This is something else. We don't need claws to finish this war. We need patience and understanding.

Light begins to spill from the woman's arms, spreading to encompass her and the phantom in her arms, the soul of what I know without a doubt is *her* baby. Somehow, Ananke once birthed and lost a child.

We all watch with wide eyes as the light grows brighter with each passing second.

"What's happening?" I whisper, hoping someone will know. I'm not surprised when it's Aniya who answers.

"Prophesy," she says softly. "It's prophesy."

"So, she was never meant to break the worlds?" Wendy asks, clear confusion in her eyes just as many of the others sport.

"She would have, but with all that power must come balance." Aniya smiles over at Wendy. "I'm the balance."

Peter gasps beside her, looking down at his daughter with new eyes. The stars were never an accident. Everything has a purpose and Aniya is a part of that, revealed by this very moment. We always have a choice in the matter, but the world must balance out with our decisions. Sometimes, those decisions are made for us.

Tink stares between Aniya and the glowing woman with wide eyes. "A child lost. A child born," she rasps.

We all shift at the realization, at the profoundness of this. Ananke lost her child only for another to be born into this world. What a cruel joke that must feel like to the woman glowing before us. How tragic. Suddenly, I understand exactly why she wanted to destroy everything. I would have wanted to do just the same. How dare the universe take her child for prophesy!

Ananke's sobs grow louder, and I choke on emotion at the sound. A high keening sound comes from her that speaks of heartbreak and loss, a tragedy she's never recovered from. I squeeze King's hand tighter as the first tear falls from my eyes. I don't think there's a dry eye in the clearing as we all watch the scene before us.

Slowly, the glow begins to fade, travelling from her knees upward. Where once there was flesh, it's replaced with stone, solidifying before our very eyes. With a final sputter, the glow disappears and a statue of a kneeling woman with a baby cradled in her arms remains. Even in death, she's protecting her child. Both souls bleed from the statue and gently float into the air, two now one. Thorny vines grow from the soil around the base of the statue, briar roses climbing along them, until they wrap around the statue gently like a final blanket of protection. A gravestone. Not a statue, at all.

"Her power?" I croak, my voice thick with the emotion of witnessing the death of someone so powerful. Not evil, just hurt.

"It will balance out," Aniya murmurs. "But before it does, the worlds will shudder. The balance is now madness." Her eyes meet mine before trailing over to Hatter. "And madness is written."

My eyes widen. "Hatter," I gasp, and he looks at first me and then Aniya.

"The baby," he gasps. "Clara."

And then he's sprinting through the trees, every single one of us following.

Madness is written. . .

Madness is written. . .

Madness. . .is written. . .

CHAPTER FIFTY-THREE

JUPITER

"Push, Clara!" I order, watching between her legs carefully. Tiger kneels beside me, both of us trying to help her as best as we can. She's fully dilated now, but the baby isn't coming out. How long has it been? I don't even know.

"How long did it take you to give birth?" I whisper to Tiger. I don't know if the magic of the worlds will quicken things along. All births are different, that much I know, but this feels different. Something is wrong.

"Not this long," Tiger murmurs. "The baby isn't crowning yet."

I look over Clara's knees to see her face pinched in pain. "I don't know if I'm doing this right," I admit.

"Just get the baby out," Clara growls. "Save the baby. Don't worry about me."

"Calm," Tiger says, her hand soothing over Clara's knee. "Remain calm. You're both going to be okay."

I kneel down again and reach up to massage Clara's stomach, trying to urge the baby to come out with the next push. "Okay, here comes the next contraction. Really big push, Clara."

Her body tenses as the contraction hits and her scream is shrill in my ears as she pushes.

"I can see the baby!" I exclaim, excitement in my voice. "That's it. Keep pushing, Clara! The baby's coming!"

"Push, Clara," Tiger repeats.

Clara's keen grows louder, pain in every level of the word, digging deep, but it's not just the pain of childbirth I realize.

I glance at Tiger. "Isn't the baby supposed to come out head first?" I ask quietly, fear in my voice.

"It is," Tiger confirms.

Horror hits me just as blood begins to spread outward from beneath Clara. Oh no! I'm no doctor but I know this is bad. Too much blood. That's too much blood! The baby is facing the wrong direction.

"Stop pushing, Clara," I command, my voice hard so she knows I mean it.

"What?" she asks, panting, her voice already weak. "What is it? What's wrong?"

"Stay calm," Tiger tells her.

"What's wrong with my baby?" Clara trembles.

"We're going to do everything we can—"

"Jupiter," she cuts me off, her voice that of the empress. "Tell me what's wrong."

I meet her eyes and know I can't keep the secret. "You're losing a lot of blood, and the baby is turned the wrong way."

Fear flickers in her eyes. "Save the baby," she orders.

"But what about you—"

"Save the baby," she repeats, her voice hard, leaving no room for argument. "Save the baby first."

But I refuse to let Clara die. I won't let her die, not on my watch. Hatter trusts us. We can't allow the Empress of Wonderland to die. We can't let one of the triad bleed out.

"What do we do?" I ask Tiger, meeting her eyes.

There's clear worry there, too, and when she shakes her head, I know she has no answers either. If we don't act fast, we're going to lose both of them.

Clara's skin almost glows with power, and if not for my panic, I might have wondered after it.

I search inside my mind for answers, trying desperately to find them, knowing there's always an answer, but instead of finding any clear answer, I find the stars instead. They swell at my acknowledgement, beckon me forward, and I move on pure instinct.

The door slams open behind us and Hatter storms in, his eyes going to the blood beneath his mate. His eyes are wide in panic and fear, and when he looks at me in desperation as the others gather in behind him, my power explodes out of me.

Time slows and stops for everyone except a few. I know which ones are immune to my power because they carry the stars themselves. Aniya, Red, Peter. . .and somehow, Hatter moves despite my power.

Sparks fly from my fingers and swirl around Clara as she lays frozen, her face pinched in pain as another contraction hits. Tiger kneels in the same position, her hand on Clara's knees in comfort. With shaking fingers, I reach forward and lay my hand on Clara's stomach, healing her even as the baby continues to push out. My sparks cushion the baby, protecting it, but it comes at a cost for Clara. Her pelvic bone snaps, but even as it does, my sparks are healing the bone, keeping her from bleeding out.

Behind us, time slowly begins to move again just as Red breaks through and stare with wide eyes at the sparks. And then my power releases everyone around us with a snap, sending them stumbling. Red's smiling, but I can't look at her and acknowledge what we are. I don't have time to. Hatter stumbles forward as I quickly wrap the baby in a blanket and wipe it clean of the blood. Tiger stands and helps despite the clear confusion between the panic and a baby suddenly in my arms. She rubs at the baby until a shrill cry fills the room, announcing the birth better than I ever can. There are so many sighs of relief, I don't know who they all come from, but when I turn toward Hatter and a living, breathing Clara with the baby in my arms, I smile even as tiny iridescent stars sparkle along the baby's skin.

"Congratulations," I croak, my voice thick with a sob at what I've just done, what my power had allowed me to do. "It's a boy. . ."

CHAPTER FIFTY-FOUR

RED

There's cause for celebration in Oz even as the worlds shift yet again. The Grimm Forest retreats but not far. More worlds move around us, organizing things in a half-hazard semblance of chaos. No one understands how things will work, if the worlds will keep shifting or if they'll settle. No one knows if they'll separate again or merge. We have no answers, but there's still cause for celebration.

Oz is safe for now.

We won and though many of us were hurt, we're still alive. Jupiter and I have been able to heal those worse off, making sure no one will have complications from the injuries.

Gillikin suffered a loss in people, much to Tin's dismay, but he'd held a large service for all those he lost while fighting for Oz. Too many brave people. Too many new graves.

A baby was born, a powerful one.

I watch as Aniya coos to the baby in Clara's arms, power meeting power. I can see the stars that dance in the baby's eyes when he looks around and I know he'll shake the worlds just as Aniya will. Ananke's power found the balance in the still unnamed baby.

King sits beside me, both of us in human form, watching everything that's transpiring. So much has changed, and yet now we have a moment to breathe, to recuperate. All three personalities King carries inside of him talk to me without restraint, no longer hiding what he is from the others. A few had asked about the three lion heads, but he doesn't shy away from the questions now. Together, we embrace everything that we are.

Briella gave me a whole wardrobe of clothing to wear, and though I miss wearing King's shirts, I love the clothing she made me even more. Everything has the crest sewn into it, sometimes hidden, sometimes front and center, and it's all so well made. Perhaps, my favorite piece, is the brilliant red cloak she gifted me. The clasp chain that holds it onto my shoulders sports golden medallions with the crest. It's a gift she doesn't understand how much it means to me, but I hugged her for it so tightly, she had to realize. I've never had so many friends before, but now, I'm surrounded by them.

"Do you regret the monster you are?" King asks suddenly from beside me, his eyes on the baby. When he looks back to me, I see longing there and I'm not sure I ever expected the Lion of Oz to want to be a father. It's not time—I know it's not—but I don't discount the idea for one day in the future. Perhaps, when fate blesses us with a child, the world will be different.

I smile at his question and shake my head. "No. I think I'm exactly the monster I'm meant to be and that's okay." I take his hand. "Being a monster is easy. Being a good monster takes work, but in the end, it's worth it."

With my free hand, I scoop up a small chunk of wood and hold it up before me. My sparks fly from my skin to shape around it, and when they fade away, the wood is in two shapes, a wolf and a three-headed lion, as if I'd carved them by hand. "The lion and the lobo," I muse, passing them into his waiting claws. "Who would have thought?"

He closes his hands around the carved figures and holds them against his chest. "You honor me, little wolf." Carefully he sets them to the side and reaches down into a bag he's taken to carrying around. "I have something for you, too."

When he pulls out the golden crown, a wolf emblazoned on the front, a match to his with three lions, I laugh happily and gently take it.

"I told you we'd make you our Queen," Fang murmurs.

"You did indeed," I whisper, staring at it.

"Here," Ophir speaks. "Allow me."

Gently, King takes the crown from my hand and together, with all three of them present, he places it on my head, crowning me right there on the yellow brick road.

"The lion and the lobo," he repeats, his eyes alight with emotion. He leans in and presses a sweet kiss against my lips. "I love you, little wolf."

The corners of my eyes crinkling, I wrap my hand around the back of his neck. "And I love you, courageous lion."

The worlds sigh and tremble, a warning of what's to come, but still, we'll be okay. We have each other as we were always meant to, and that's all that matters.

Even if when monsters fall in love, the whole universe trembles at their feet. . .

EPILOGUE

RUMPELSTILTSKIN

I'm running, sprinting through trees that reach for my clothing and tears the fabric. I'm scrambling through the Grimm Forest, a place that used to be home, a world that I once felt as if I belonged to, but I belong nowhere. Not anymore. I'm a trickster, a misplaced enchanter, and there's no world that would dare to want me.

I only need to get away from Oz, away from Ananke and Toto, away from the danger that lives in that direction. She'll either lose or she'll win, but I know I just need to keep moving despite the rumbling of the worlds beneath my feet.

In the distance, a banshee shrieks and I curse under my breath.

Run, run, run, keeping running. Don't stop until you're safe.

I cut through the tree line and leap over the flowing river, landing on the other side in mud that squelches in my shoes. I don't pay it any mind. I have to get out. I have to keep moving.

Run, run, run!

A stick snaps behind me, a warning, and I freeze. If I'm hearing the sound, whoever is there wants me to know they're there. I don't turn, not yet, waiting for them to reveal themselves.

"Well, hello, Lord Rumpelstiltskin," the voice purrs. "I've been looking for you."

With a heavy sigh of defeat, I hold up my hands in surrender.

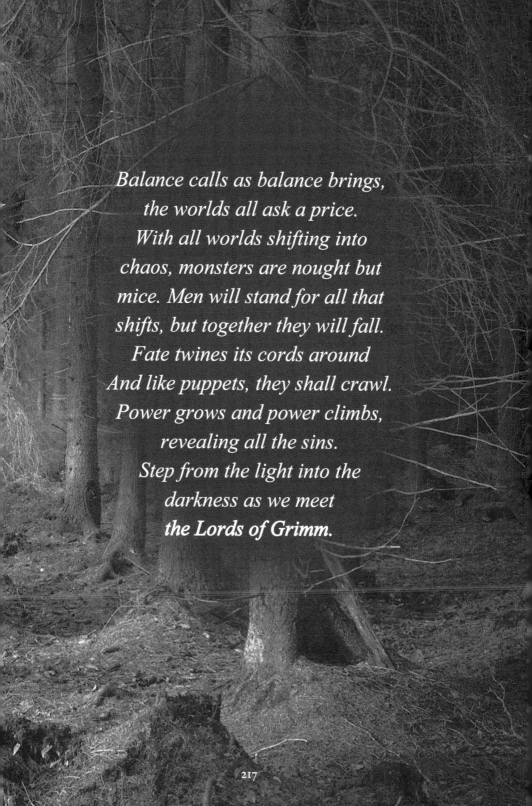

Balance calls as balance brings,
the worlds all ask a price.
With all worlds shifting into
chaos, monsters are nought but
mice. Men will stand for all that
shifts, but together they will fall.
Fate twines its cords around
And like puppets, they shall crawl.
Power grows and power climbs,
revealing all the sins.
Step from the light into the
darkness as we meet
the Lords of Grimm.

To continue the adventure...

Grab Vengeful as a Beauty now!
Books2read.com/vengefulasabeauty

About the Author

Kendra Moreno is secretly a spy but when she's not dealing in secrets and espionage, you can find her writing her latest adventure. She lives in Texas where the summer days will make you melt, and southern charm comes free with every meal. She's a recovering Road Rager (kind of) and slowly overcoming her Star Wars addiction (nope!), and she definitely didn't pass on her addiction to her son (she did). She has one hellhound named Mayhem who got tired of guarding the Gates of Hell and now guards her home against monsters. She's a geek, a mother, a scuba diver, a tyrannosaurus rex, and a wordsmith who sometimes switches out her pen for a sword.

If you see Kendra on the streets, don't worry: you can distract her with talks about Kylo Ren or Loki.
#LokiLives #BringBackBenSolo

To find out more about Kendra, you can check her out on her website or join her
Facebook group, Kendra's World of Wonder.
Sign up for Kendra's Newsletter:
https://mailchi.mp/feb46d2b29ad/babbleandquill

facebook.com/AuthorKendraMoreno
twitter.com/KendramorenoA
instagram.com/kendramorenoauthor
bookbub.com/authors/kendra-moreno

Made in the USA
Las Vegas, NV
25 October 2024

10350538R00134